THE GRUMP

THE LEBLANC BROTHERS
LAYLA HAGEN

CONTENTS

Chapter One
Xander

"Xander, your grandparents are here," my assistant, Lydia, said, poking her head into my office.

"Great. Bring them in, please."

She smiled, looking a bit unsure of herself, which wasn't like her at all. Then again, my grandparents—especially my grandmothers—could be a bit intimidating for those who didn't know them well.

As they stepped into my office, I was overwhelmed with pride to be their grandson.

David and Isabeau LeBlanc and Celine and Felix Broussard were pillars of the Orleans Conglomerate. My five brothers and I were running the businesses now, after Dad ran it for decades, and we did so very successfully. But they were the reason the company had lasted for so many generations.

"So glad you could make time to come."

"It's not every day that the four of us are summoned into one of our grandsons' offices. Do we have a reason to worry, darling?" Celine asked.

The two families were at odds once upon a time—they'd been rivals in business and dead set against my parents marrying—but now they were very tight.

"No, not at all."

"I still don't know why you don't have an office in the French Quarter like everyone else," Felix said, strolling to the window.

I'd chosen the financial district as my home base, with no regrets. "I can focus better here," I replied honestly. "For me, the Quarter is for fun, not for working."

"I quite like the view," David exclaimed. He was sitting in one of the four chairs I'd arranged in front of my desk. "Since you asked us here, I'm assuming you mean business?"

I nodded. The Orleans Conglomerate was a vast enterprise that was doing extremely well. We dabbled in a lot of things, from shipping to restaurants, bakeries to bars, and several other types of businesses in between.

"As I told you before, I aim to make the Orleans Conglomerate as profitable as possible." I leaned forward with my elbows on my desk, hoping they'd agree with what I was about to suggest.

"Yes," Isabeau said in a warning tone. I bet she already knew where I was going with this.

"It's about the confectionery, isn't it?" Celine said, sighing.

I'd already mentioned this to them once before, in passing. But now I'd actually crunched the numbers properly, and that business had to go.

I looked from one grandparent to another, ending with Celine. The confectionery business was something she and Isabeau had started together years ago, which was why I wanted to break this to them face-to-face.

"I've been running the numbers, and several of our businesses aren't profitable. The confectionery is the worst offender."

Celine looked down at her hands as Isabeau sighed. "Oh, my boy. That was a passion project that Celine and I started years ago."

"I know that," I chimed in with as gentle a voice as I could, "but it makes no sense to keep it going."

David looked at his wife and then turned to me. "Grandson, we can't tell you what to do or not to do. You know the deal in our family. When someone chooses to retire, they also give up any decision rights."

"I know, but I wanted to discuss this with you all, as I didn't want it to come as a shock." I found their approach very smart. Too many decision-makers could lead to problems, and with all my brothers, it was tough enough as it was.

We'd been successful with the way we were managing different branches of the business so no one would step on anyone's toes. I was the self-appointed CFO. I'd gotten into it by mistake, and I realized I liked working with numbers. They were black-and-white and told a clean-cut story. My ambition was to make the Orleans Conglomerate the most profitable it had ever been. That was the main reason I didn't make decisions with my emotions. Some business branches had sentimental value to my grandparents, I knew. For me, they were simply relics of times past.

"What do you intend to do?" Celine asked.

"I haven't totally decided yet. The easiest thing would be to just sell it off."

"But we've put so much work into it," Isabeau said.

"Careful, grandson. They're going to start with a guilt trip," David cautioned.

I laughed. "It's their prerogative."

"It makes no sense to keep it. It never did," Isabeau sighed. "But it was something we enjoyed doing."

"You want to sell it *now*?" Celine asked, clearly affronted.

"Well, that's a good point, dear. With Christmas peeping around the corner, it's the busiest time for the business," Isabeau added.

"The numbers are strongest this time of year. They make the most pralines around Christmas," I said.

"*We* make the most pralines," Isabeau corrected. It was obvious that these two were still invested in the business.

"Let me assess it all and see what's best. Nothing will happen around Christmastime, as everyone is too busy ending their year to scout for new businesses."

"Have you ever been to the confectionery?" Isabeau asked.

"No, Isabeau, I haven't." I didn't have time to visit businesses that didn't even cover their costs.

"Do pay a visit," Celine said, "but after we do! We'd like to tell the LeCarre girls in person that things might change."

"I was going to take a look at the place anyway. It's part of the assessment."

That seemed to appease them a bit, until Isabeau shook her head and said, "One of these days, I hope you'll grow a heart, young man. Now you've got a stone."

Oh boy.

"Isabeau, don't be like that," Celine chastised. "Xander simply wants to improve profits. There's nothing wrong with that."

"I agree," David said. I could always count on the grandfathers.

I looked at him. "You know, I'm surprised this business survived all these years. Especially after Dad took it over."

David started to laugh. "Xander, one day you'll realize that even the toughest man wants to keep his wife happy. Always been my motto, and Felix's too. 'Happy wife, happy life.' These two were happy as clams out there at their confectionery, messing around with chocolate recipes. They kept saying it was their way of blowing off steam, which never made sense to me. It's just exchanging one kitchen for the other."

"It's not even remotely the same," Isabeau countered.

"These two always left us to our own devices," Celine said with affection. "And your dad..."

"Well, he has a bit more heart than you," Isabeau went on.

I was laughing in earnest now. "Isabeau, this is more guilt-tripping than I was expecting from you, I have to admit."

"The Orleans Conglomerate is very successful. I don't see how having a branch or two that don't perform is going to hurt that much," she replied.

"It's about the principle. Anything that bleeds money needs to be cut off."

Isabeau shook her head theatrically. "Oh, Xander. You truly are hopeless."

"I'll take that as a compliment." Where everyone saw me as cutthroat, I saw myself as precise. When they said I was hopeless, I knew I was focused.

There were only so many hours in a day; there was no point in dabbling in stuff that wasn't worth the effort.

"Well, thank you for telling us," Celine said. "Your secretary mentioned that you have another meeting starting in... oh, look at that, five minutes, so we'd best get a move on."

"She said that?" I was stunned.

"I believe the implication was that we shouldn't overstay our welcome."

My assistant knows I like to keep things on schedule and probably just said that as a normal reaction.

"I'm sorry. That's true for everyone except family. You're welcome to stay longer."

"But then we'd be interrupting your meeting," Isabeau countered.

"Yes, but it can wait."

"Just promise me something," Isabeau said. "You'll go out to the LeBlanc-Broussard confectionery with an open mind and look at everything they've been doing. The business brings people joy."

"I'll keep an open mind," I said, but it was more for their sake. There was no possibility of my seeing anything there that would tell another story than the financial one. "Are you heading to the Quarter? I can join you for drinks later."

"We're going back to the perfume shop, of course," Celine said briskly.

"Of course you are." I smiled at both of my grandmothers.

After retiring, the two of them opened a fragrance shop on Decatur Street. They spent most of their days there.

"If you're buying, I can definitely take a walk around until everyone's done with work," David said cheerfully.

Unlike their other halves, he and Felix had decided that once they left the family business, they wanted to dedicate their entire retirement to fishing. Which they had so far.

"But seriously, Xander, you should get to know Avery and Bailey," Celine said.

"I think you'll quite like the LeCarre girls," Isabeau added.

That was neither here nor there. Me liking or disliking the employees in charge of any of the businesses wasn't going to sway my decision.

"Right. We'll be going, then," Isabeau concluded.

Her tone was a little bit chillier than usual, but I was expecting that. I probably could've broken the news in a gentler manner, but I wasn't very good at that. This was how I operated.

"You know, Bella won't be very happy about it," she continued. "She loves the pralines."

Now *that* was a low blow because I had a soft spot for my niece. She'd been the first baby in the family. Now my brother Chad had recently welcomed another baby girl—Simone—with his fiancée.

"I'll make sure she still gets them," I assured her as they left the office.

My family was tight-knit, and we were always honest with one another. It was what I always told Bella—no matter the situation, honesty would win.

That little girl had held my heart since the moment she was born, and now she was almost ten years old. Her two passions in life were beignets and Harry Potter. I couldn't really do much about the latter, but I helped with the former as often as possible.

Isabeau's words came back to me: *"Bella won't be very happy about it."*

Leave it to Isabeau to fight as dirty as possible. But she wasn't going to sway me. Nothing would, not even meeting Avery and her sister, Bailey. Only the numbers mattered.

Chapter Two

Bailey

"And another batch done!" I exclaimed.

"You're on a roll today," Avery said.

I peeked at her table. We were always in a bit of a competition. "I cheated," I said. "I put myself in a good mood—that always gives me an extra boost of energy."

Avery laughed. "You think I didn't realize that was your strategy when I came in this morning and you had carols playing already? It's not even Thanksgiving, woman."

I shrugged, mouthing the lyrics. I swear I knew the lyrics for every song ever written for Christmas. Personally, I found Christmas in New Orleans to be the best thing ever. Most people, tourists especially, came to the city for Mardi Gras, and that was spectacular as well. But it was extra magical around Christmas. It was also our busiest time, which meant I couldn't fully enjoy the season the way I wanted to. But that was a good problem to have.

"Since I did such good work, I'm going to reward myself." I took a praline from the tray in front of me, popped it into my mouth, and sighed. "I think this new recipe is going to be a success."

"I agree. You truly do have a knack for coming up with new recipes."

"They come easily to me. It's like I wake up in the morning and can practically feel the taste in my mouth. And it ends up tasting exactly the way I imagined."

Avery winked. "Thank goodness you have the creative gene. I'm just good at executing."

We both truly loved our work. Some days I still couldn't believe I was making chocolates for a living, but I wasn't going to look a gift horse in the mouth.

"By the way, I forgot to tell you. Isabeau and Celine are visiting today."

I almost choked on half of the praline. "What? When?"

"I spoke to Celine this morning, and it totally slipped my mind."

"When are they coming?"

She checked the clock. "One hour, give or take."

I jumped to my feet. "That still gives me time to make some of their favorites, and we do have that sherry they both love."

Avery laughed. "I'm sorry. I should've told you before. You always get frenzied when they visit."

"I know, but I like to spoil them. They're so good to us."

"Yes, they are."

"All right. Do we have pistachio?" I muttered to myself even though I knew we did. Celine absolutely loved my pistachio recipe. Isabeau was more traditional. Her favorites were the sherry pralines, and we always had plenty of those. The two of them hadn't visited in a while, and I was ecstatic to see them. "Let's get to work."

"Need my help?" Avery asked.

"No, you finish doing your thing."

"Thanks."

Celine and Isabeau were two spectacular women. The confectionery made pralines for all of the LeBlanc & Broussard establishments. They were sought after on their restaurants' dessert menus and sometimes served with drinks at the bar. We also gave away a lot to charity, especially now during the Christmas season. We had several visits planned at local kids' hospitals. Celine liked to say that the LeBlanc-Broussard confectionery was spreading joy, and I quite agreed with her. I personally thought we had the best pralines in the city, and that was saying something because competition was fierce in New Orleans.

I whipped up everything I needed for the pistachio pralines in twenty minutes and shoved them into the oven, then started preparing a platter with small bites. Nothing fancy, just charcuterie. It was what Avery and I had for lunch almost every day. Both Celine and Isabeau had liked it the last time I offered it to them.

I kept an eye on the clock, but things were going smoothly.

When I had five minutes to go, Avery asked, "Want to freshen up?" She had just put on some lipstick and combed her hair. Avery and I looked a lot alike. We were both petite, but her hair was much thicker than mine. I was also a bit curvy from all the pralines—but my mantra was that life is too short to forgo pralines.

"You read my mind," I told my sister, then kissed her cheek for good measure before heading to the bathroom.

Another of my favorite parts about work was that I was spending all of my time with my sister. We were a small team, with only two other employees to run errands for us and help with packaging, but mostly it was just the two of us. The confectionery wasn't big enough to warrant more personnel. We were at the outskirts of the city in a small redbrick building with large windows. All of our gorgeous packaging with the LeBlanc & Broussard logo on it was stored in a separate room. Even though the company had been renamed the Orleans Conglomerate a long time ago, I was happy that they didn't change the logo for the boxes. "Conglomerate" felt cold and faceless, but having the family names on the boxes was completely different. "LeBlanc & Broussard" seemed upscale and more personal.

I inspected myself in the mirror. First step, I let my hair down so it fell in messy dark brown curls, then ran my hand through it a few times until I was happy with the look of it. I didn't bother wearing makeup at all at work because it would simply melt off. But every time these two were visiting, I felt severely underdressed and under accessorized. They were always so put together—true Southern ladies, all style with no attitude. So I put on my favorite lipstick and some mascara.

When I opened the door to the bathroom, I heard Isabeau's distinctive voice. Celine was laughing with my sister. I hoped to convince them to stop by more often.

"And you have the sherry ready. Oh, these girls, they're something else," Celine said.

"Hi," I greeted, stepping into the kitchen.

"My darling," Isabeau exclaimed. They both kissed my cheek.

"I'll have pistachio pralines ready in a minute," I told them.

"You didn't have to bother for us," Celine said, but her tone was distinctively appreciative.

"If you come all the way here, the least I can do is have your favorites ready."

"I forgot to tell her you were stopping by," Avery said as she poured sherry into two glasses.

Isabeau and Celine clinked them together, and then Isabeau said, "You've got chorizo again. I bought some for home too."

"The boys love it as well," Celine said.

I barely bit down a chuckle. It always surprised me when they referred to their seventy-year-old husbands as "boys." Though I suppose in their eyes, they were the same young men they'd once fallen in love with.

I took out the pralines and said, "These need to cool a bit."

"Chorizo is severely underused in Louisiana," Celine said.

"True. We pumped up the jambalaya with it, and it's been a success," Isabeau added.

"I've poured sherry for us too," Avery said to me.

"Avery," I chastised, "it's the middle of the workday."

"A little bit of sherry helps with inspiration," Celine said in a conspiratorial tone, but she and Isabeau exchanged a glance that made me feel uneasy.

"Sure, thank you," I told my sister.

She was right, and besides, it was delicious. We only ever opened it when these two came to visit. Avery had poured much less for us, and I took a bite of cheese, too, to have something in my stomach—well, besides the several pralines I'd eaten throughout the day.

I watched the two of them intently. Celine leaned forward, opening her mouth as though she intended to say something, but then settled back in the chair. She was hesitating. This was unusual, and I felt like it wasn't good. I glanced at my sister, but she was happily sipping from her glass. She clearly hadn't noticed anything. Maybe I was imagining things. Then Isabeau cleared her throat, and my stomach bottomed out.

"Listen, girls, we have a reason for stopping by today."

"You have more ideas for the Christmas recipes?" Avery asked. "Because the ones you had last year were an absolute hit."

Isabeau shook her head. "Unfortunately, no. As you know, we officially retired from running the company or having anything to do with it a long time ago."

"Yes. We know that," I said.

"And then so did my son."

I frowned. We already knew all of this. "Sure. Your grandchildren are running it now, and as far as we've heard, they're doing a fabulous job."

I'd met some of them over the years, especially around Christmas when the LeBlanc-Broussard mansion was part of the Holiday Home tours.

"Yes. Well, you might not know that Xander is the CFO," Celine explained.

I furrowed my brow. "I don't think I've met Xander."

"I did a couple of times," Avery said. "But we've only exchanged a few words."

"Anyway, he's been going over the financials, and..." Isabeau shook her head. "I can't say it."

I felt as if someone had pulled the rug from under me. Isabeau didn't shy away from difficult situations. She faced them head-on. I'd gathered that much from all the stories she regaled us with from her time in the company. So if she couldn't even bring herself to say it...

"What is it?" I asked softly.

Celine looked at Avery and then at me. "Well, he wants to sell off the confectionery."

"S-S-Sell off? What is there to sell?" I questioned before I could help myself.

Celine shrugged. "We told him it's always been a passion project. Our goal was to bring a little more joy to the customers of our other businesses and to all of the charities in New Orleans."

"Exactly," I said. I was having trouble processing this at the moment, and it had nothing to do with the sherry.

"But he insists that it would make more sense to simply buy pralines from somewhere else instead of producing them."

I couldn't breathe. I pressed a hand on my chest and tried again, but somehow, air wouldn't come into my lungs.

"I see," Avery said. "That's very unfortunate." My sister glanced at me, and I could see my own sadness reflected in her eyes.

"It is," Celine replied. "We've tried to persuade him not to do it. He'll be around here sometime soon to take a look. Nothing is set in stone."

"Except his heart," Isabeau muttered.

Celine cut her eyes to Isabeau, then went on. "Xander is very stubborn, but I think you could change his mind."

"I might not have met Xander, but I've heard stories about him," I confessed. "He doesn't seem like the type who changes his mind once he decides on something."

"That's just the thing," Celine said. "We're not sure if he's actually decided or is just toying with the idea."

"Oh, Celine, tell the girls the truth," Isabeau admonished, then turned to me. "He did seem pretty firm with his decision."

"But you told him that most of our business is for charity, right?" I pleaded.

"Yes, he knows," Celine said. "He insists that we can continue doing our charity even with buying the pralines somewhere else."

"But we have unique recipes," I countered. "Some of the favorites can't even be found anywhere else."

"We didn't get into specifics with him," Isabeau said, "but I'm certain you two can."

"He's never been here before, so maybe once he sees this place, he'll cherish it as much as we do," Celine added, but she sounded as if she didn't believe herself either.

My heart was pounding fast in my chest. "Did he say when he's planning to do all this?"

"After Christmas," Isabeau said. "He said that any potential buyer will be busy during the holiday season. But I do think he'll drop by soon."

I let out a breath of relief. "So at least we have this Christmas season. That's good because I've promised the staff at the children's hospital that we'll drop by with some of their favorites. I'd hate to disappoint them."

"I think this Christmas is safe," Isabeau assured us.

"Just a word of warning," Celine said. "Xander is a bit of a grump."

"Celine, why aren't you being straightforward with these two today? He's very much a grump, nothing 'a bit' about it. He's all about the numbers, if something is profitable, yada, yada, yada. But he's very good at what he does, and he's very loyal to the family. We love him to bits, but he's a bit too calculated for his own good."

"Or ours," Avery murmured under her breath.

"Girls, you have nothing to worry about. We'll write stellar recommendations for you, if it comes to that," Isabeau promised.

"I'm sure you'll find fantastic jobs... if necessary," Celine added.

"Yes, even within our restaurants as pastry chefs. We'll figure out something for you ladies."

"Thank you," Avery said politely.

I couldn't properly form words. Of course I was grateful, but neither of us truly wanted that.

Neither my sister nor I had a traditional pastry chef's education. We'd actually both been software developers up until a few years ago. I threw all I had into building my career, and then one day, it simply got to be too much. I took a break, assuming that after a few months, I'd start job hunting again. One day, I saw a conversion course for pastry chefs. I signed up for it mostly for fun and discovered I absolutely loved it. I'd been hooked ever since.

Avery signed up with me at the same time even though she was still working back then. Isabeau was our teacher, and on the last day of the course, she told us about the confectionery and how the old chefs were retiring. I couldn't even remember how she convinced us to stop by, but we did. We were charmed by everything: the thick willow tree in front of the building; the cozy feeling of baking; the fact that we only had to make pralines, which wouldn't require too much experience.

The salary hadn't been much to brag about, but we'd started a business on the side, making online videos for amateur bakers—an online academy of sorts. Between the two, I was making a very good income. I even bought my own house.

But if the confectionery closed, things would change. I wasn't that worried about money, at least not in the short-term. We wouldn't be left destitute, as we could definitely continue to grow the online business. My parents instilled in us a solid work ethic, and from the get-go, we had a very comfortable, middle-class upbringing. Mom was still a nurse, and Dad had been a salesman, retiring a few years ago when his health declined. We had a lot of fun on family trips growing up, mostly camping. My parents were my role models in life, and I longed for a love like the one they had.

But I loved being here at the confectionery. It was exactly what I wanted to do with the rest of my life. And now that might not happen.

Isabeau clapped her hands together. "So, now that we got that out of the way, why don't you tell us what new recipes you've planned for this Christmas season?"

I took another sip of sherry to get some of that good mood back. "Nougat. It was a hit three years ago, and I'm pairing it with cinnamon and star anise. It's delicious. If I knew you were coming, I would've made a tasting tray out of everything. But we could decide on another day, and I'll make it for you when you come."

"Yes, we could do that," Celine said. "But we don't want to inconvenience you."

"Nonsense," Avery said. "We'll never be too busy for the two of you."

"Then we'll gladly stop by," Isabeau said. "Actually, you know what our biggest hit was back in the day?"

"What?" I leaned slightly over the table in earnest. It was a pity these two didn't want to be in the kitchen anymore because they were immensely talented.

"You won't believe it, but it was a mix of mint and banana."

"No way," I gasped.

"Yes way," Isabeau replied with a wink. "And I came across it by accident. I'll tell you everything."

I was getting giddy as Isabeau shared her story. Oh, why didn't they come later in the day? Then we could finish this bottle of sherry and not care how tipsy we got. Sherry always paired perfectly with their stories.

As she went on explaining how her husband had eaten all the cherries she'd planned to use, so she had to resort to bananas instead, I was starting to feel more optimistic. Xander was *their* grandson. How different could he be from them? I was certain that once he came here and understood what we truly did, he'd change his mind.

Chapter Three

Xander

November and December were some of the busiest times in the office. We were watching numbers more closely than usual, and I was on top of everything. That was why I usually didn't get home until well into the evening. But unlike my brother Julian, I enjoyed spending all my time at work. Everything was calm and orderly. Julian said being cooped up in the office drove him mad, which was why he went into his flagship bar in the French Quarter a few times a week.

But even though I had a million things to do, I left the office at three o'clock the next Wednesday. I'd promised my grandmothers that I'd see the confectionery, and I intended to keep that promise. Besides, I hadn't been joking. I really did want to get a feel for it before I pitched it to a potential buyer. Or closed its doors.

Lydia jerked her head back when she saw me with my coat. "You're leaving?"

"Yes. I'm heading to the confectionery. There's nothing else on my schedule, right?" She looked so shocked that I wondered if I'd forgotten about something.

"No, no. As I told you, the team from Dallas couldn't come because they all have the flu."

"Unfortunate, but perfect. Call me if anything urgent comes up."

"Sure." She still sounded perplexed. I didn't blame her. Even when meetings were canceled, I rarely left the office unless my niece or my family needed me for some reason. Otherwise, I was behind my desk until at least six or seven o'clock.

I put the confectionery's address in the GPS and groaned. Why the fuck was it so far away? Then again, that was why the building they were in had been so cheap. It would be a good asset to sell to anyone interested. I was already making up a pitch in my mind. I knew the numbers by heart, which was both a blessing and a curse for me—once I saw numbers, I couldn't forget them.

Even though it was a very small operation, it could be a good add-on for someone already in the chocolate industry. Any buyer worth his salt would see that.

The drive didn't take as long as I initially thought it would. The redbrick building looked solid enough. I immediately viewed it from a buyer's perspective, and no immediate investments were needed. My grandmothers called this place "charming," but all I could see was a waste of money. I was all about honoring legacy, but the Orleans Conglomerate needed to be brought into the modern era.

I stepped through the front gate into a huge yard and blinked. *Are those twinkle lights?* I was pretty sure that's what Bella called them—and they were everywhere. There was also a huge willow tree in the center and about a million ferns scattered throughout the area.

I stepped forward, looking for the entrance, and immediately found it. It was cracked open, and Christmas carols were filtering out. It was the first time I'd heard them this season, and in my opinion, it was far too early.

"Hello? Anyone here?" I asked, knocking at the front door.

"Who is it? It's just me, Bailey, here. Everyone else has left for the day."

That's how she announces herself? Is she inviting people to rob her?

"It's Xander LeBlanc."

"Oh." Her reaction told me that my grandmothers had already informed her of everything. "Come in."

The place smelled like oranges and a lot of other things I couldn't pinpoint. I'd never had a very *discerning* nose, as Isabeau would say.

I followed the sound of pans and whatnot until I came to what was obviously a kitchen. I immediately took stock of the six stoves. Only two were currently working.

"I'll be finished with this right away," Bailey said.

My eyes widened when I caught side of her, surprised at how gorgeous she was. Her dark brown hair was in a lopsided ponytail. I couldn't see the color of her eyes from here, but the shape of her mouth was exquisite.

Fuck! What has gotten into me? I didn't normally notice things like that when I was inspecting a business.

"Okay, now it's done." She put the bowl down and straightened up. Her eyes were impossibly green. *Is she wearing colored contacts?* "I'm Bailey LeCarre. Your grandmothers said you were going to stop by but didn't mention when."

"I decided on a whim to come today."

"As I said, it's just me right now. Everyone else already left for the day."

"At four o'clock?" I asked incredulously.

She narrowed her eyes. "They had errands to run. They didn't just go home to rest."

I'd clearly come on too strong. I didn't want to antagonize her, but something about her was throwing me off my game.

She pointed to the bowl. "If you give me a few minutes, I'll put this in the oven. Then we can talk and I can show you around."

"Sounds good."

"Do you want anything to drink? We prepare snacks for your grandmothers when they come by, but since I didn't know..."

That was thoughtful. Isabeau and Celine loved snacks.

"I'm good. I'll just wait for you to finish."

I was having trouble keeping my eyes on hers instead of her mouth and... other parts of her body. She moved around efficiently, and only five minutes later, she shoved a trayful of pralines into the oven.

She turned around, giving a small smile. "I'm all yours."

Fuck me! I could imagine her saying that sentence while lying in my bed—

What the hell? I had no idea what had gotten into me. Instant lust or attraction wasn't part of my vocabulary. I was far too logical for that.

"What exactly did my grandmothers tell you?" I asked.

Her smile fell, and she held her arms out at her sides. "That you plan to sell this off."

"This operation isn't making a profit. You have to know that, right?"

"Yes, of course. But your grandmothers always insisted that this place wasn't made to be profitable. I mean, we're not *selling* our products to anyone. It's only used internally for business, or charity. How do you even measure profits in this case?"

It was a genuine question.

"Well, since there's no income, I simply look at the costs and—"

"It would be cheaper if you just bought the pralines from somewhere else," she finished for me.

"Exactly."

"I see. Well, let me show you around and tell you a bit about the business. I don't know how much you know."

"Not a lot," I admitted. "I just follow what the numbers say."

Her smile fell again. "The numbers? Xander, this place is..." She shook her head. "Never mind." She turned to the side so I could see past her. "Well, this is the kitchen. My sister and I are the chefs, but it's really just the two of us, so we have no one to preside over. It gets a bit tricky around Christmas when we've got a lot of orders, but that's when the errand guys we have also pitch in. The ovens are state of the art. We bought them a few years ago."

"Were they really necessary?" I couldn't help myself. That had been on my mind ever since I'd seen the purchase in our records.

Her eyes turned steely. I was somehow managing to make this Christmas carol lover/candy maker mad at me. "They're far more efficient as far as electricity goes. And the other ones were old as dirt. They weren't even baking evenly anymore, which is very important when you're making pralines."

"Fair enough. It's not my area of expertise."

She gave me a smile that obviously meant *"Clearly,"* then walked toward a small door. "Through here is our pantry." She opened it, and I could see a vast space filled from floor to ceiling with jars. "The next room is what I call our assembly room, but it's basically just a room with boxes where we pack the pralines before delivering them."

"And that delivery couldn't be outsourced?"

She replied in a rather brusque tone, "As I said before, they also double as kitchen helpers during rush season. All the boxes you see here are for Christmas. Throughout the year we use others. It depends on what kind of charity we're taking the pralines to, or if any of your restaurants and bars have a celebration. My favorites are the boxes we donate to the children's hospital. The kids are always so happy to get our pralines."

I could tell she really cared about this place. "How long have you been doing this?"

"Seven years."

"And both you and your sister went to culinary school?"

"Pastry school," she said.

"Right. So, this isn't really a good use of your skills, is it?"

She bristled. "We make the best pralines in town. I'd say it's an excellent use of our degrees."

"I didn't mean to insult you," I assured her. "If I end up selling this off and the next owner wants to bring in his own team, you'd be free to work in a bigger establishment. Surely the aspiration of any chef would be to work in a bigger kitchen, right?"

"I happen to be quite happy with how things are, Xander. I love life at the confectionery. But clearly you and I have different ideas about—" She gave me a sad smile. "—everything. But we do at least have this Christmas season, right? That's what your grandmothers said."

"Yes, of course. I know this is the busiest season. I wouldn't close down operations now. I'll keep an eye on things and make a decision after."

Her eyes suddenly turned warm. "So, it's not definitive yet?"

"I promised my grandmothers that I'll think this through thoroughly, so that's what I'll do."

I was surprised she was so passionate about this. I'd figured it was just a job. But I was even more surprised by my reaction to her.

"All right, then. Well, it's best if you give me a heads-up if you plan to drop by again or whatever 'keeping an eye on' involves. That way I can make sure you can meet the rest of the team as well."

"Will do. Can you give me your phone number?"

"Sure."

I gave her my phone, and she immediately typed it in. Her hands looked so damn soft. I was tempted to find an excuse to touch them and see if they were as exquisite as they look.

Stop, damn it! Until the next time I saw her, I had to get myself together. I always acted professionally. *Always.*

Now I was in danger of doing the exact opposite. And that wouldn't do.

Chapter Four
Bailey

I'd been wrong about Xander LeBlanc. How on earth did I think he couldn't be too different from his grandmothers? I swear he must have been adopted. The guy wasn't anything like anyone I'd met from his family. He was definitely a grump, plus coldhearted and stubborn.

The next morning when Avery came into the kitchen, she took one glance at me and said, "Your spark is gone."

"What?" I asked, confused.

"You didn't put on Christmas carols. You look like you're lost in your thoughts, and not the good kind. What's wrong?"

I sighed. "I'd planned to tell you this over lunch, but I'll just rip off the Band-Aid."

She grimaced. "Don't scare me."

"Xander paid a visit yesterday."

"Xander LeBlanc?"

"The one and only."

"He dropped by unannounced? Ballsy of him." That made me laugh. "You should've called me."

"Why?"

"Because I've already met the guy once when I took pralines to the LeBlanc-Broussard restaurant. He's an acquired taste."

That made me laugh even more. "You could say that."

"Although, I do remember him being quite good-looking. Though that's not saying much. I swear to God, all the LeBlanc guys are drop-dead gorgeous. They could be Hollywood stars."

"I agree with that," I said, focusing on the batter. What was there not to like about Xander LeBlanc? He was probably six feet, with thick dark hair and very penetrating eyes. "I wouldn't kick him out of bed... if he weren't such a grump trying to shut down the operation."

My sister came closer. "He actually said that?"

I looked up at her, setting down the batter bowl. "No. He said he'll 'assess things,' but I could practically feel his disdain for this place. Like he was looking around and constantly thinking, 'This is just a waste of money. And this is just a waste of money.' He said he'll keep an eye on things, and we're set for this Christmas anyway."

"Right," Avery said, taking out ingredients for more batter.

"But you know what? Maybe this will be a good opportunity to convince him that our work is important."

Avery smiled from ear to ear. "Nothing can dampen your optimism, can it?"

"No, but really," I went on, managing to hype myself up, "just think about it. He probably sits in his office all day, looking at numbers and trying to make decisions based on that. As far as I understood, unlike his brothers, he isn't in charge of a full branch. He's not a hands-on type of person. But if he watches us closely, sees what we do and how much joy our business brings people, maybe he'll change his mind."

Avery grimaced.

"Stop making that face," I chastised.

"I'm sorry. But I don't think that's how Xander operates. As far as I've heard, the guy is a genius with numbers. He managed to raise the profits of the company exponentially. Not that it wasn't doing well before, but now it's performing even better."

I deflated a bit at that. "He raised profits, huh? By cutting off other branches like ours?"

She shrugged. "I honestly don't know any details."

I bit my lower lip, thinking hard. "We've encountered skeptics in our career, and we won them over with the pralines."

"That was different, and you know it," my sister said as we both got to work on our respective batters. We had plenty of kitchen machinery, of course, but some things still had to be done by hand. "We've had great success bribing guards with pralines to let us stay past visiting hours in the hospital. Convincing Xander LeBlanc not to shut this down is different."

True, those weren't comparable, but I couldn't help being optimistic. As the day went on, I kept thinking about ways I could prove to Xander that the confectionery business was valuable. I just had to show him how much love went into this and how much joy it brought to people. Surely that had to count for something.

In the afternoon, I sat down in the small makeshift office I'd built in the corridor between the two rooms and opened my laptop.

"Oh no."

"What?" Avery called.

"Jack is sick this week. I'm taking on the deliveries."

"I can do it."

"Nah, I'm fine. Besides, it'll give me a chance to see how things have changed at the LeBlanc & Broussard restaurant since they brought on the new chef. You were there last Christmas, but I haven't gone for eons."

"Do you know she's actually engaged to Chad LeBlanc?"

My eyes widened. "No, I didn't know that. Wow, that's something. And how do you know all the gossip?"

"Isabeau likes to talk about the family."

My sister and I were very tight, but I couldn't imagine how it would be to have such a big extended family as well. We'd only met our grandparents from our dad's side a few times because they lived in Florida and were already elderly when we were born. Our parents toyed with the idea of sending us there for the summer, but they were too frail to deal with two rambunctious girls. We'd been close to Mom's parents, though.

I carefully checked all of my emails, and one in particular caught my attention. It was from Xander LeBlanc.

Title: Update Needed

Hi Bailey,

Thank you for taking your time to give me a tour. I'd like a spreadsheet with all the orders and all your production costs for this Christmas season. The one we have isn't detailed enough, and it's five years old, so it's not adjusted for inflation.

My heart grew heavy. I'd been totally wrong. There was no winning him over.

I groaned.

"What is it?" Avery asked, running to me.

I pointed to the screen. "Read it for yourself."

She leaned over my shoulder and narrowed her eyes at the screen, then half groaned, half laughed. "Told you! This guy isn't going to be swayed by us."

"That doesn't mean I'll stop trying."

Xander

Numbers were my bread and butter. And I didn't like the ones Bailey sent me at all. I'd done predictions adjusted for inflation from the information I had from five years ago, but this year, we were going to be even more in the red than usual.

Damn it, I should just close down the whole thing now. Why did I promise my grandmothers to keep it running for the Christmas season?

I glanced at the second spreadsheet she'd sent me. It was a schedule of some sort. At first I thought she'd included it by mistake, so I went over her email again.

Hi Xander,

Attached is the spreadsheet you asked for. I'm also sending you a list of all the places where we're taking pralines this year. I hope to see you at some of those events. I won't be everywhere in person, of course, but I marked the places where I will be.

I looked at the schedule again. They were delivering to LeBlanc & Broussard today at seven o'clock. I could make it there in time. She wasn't the one bringing the pralines, which made sense. But it would serve me well to meet someone else on the team and see what exactly the delivery process was all about.

For the rest of the afternoon, I focused on more pressing matters, such as where we were on the profit and loss prediction so far. I insisted on being part of the planning in all of the Orleans Conglomerate businesses every year. It was a hellish amount of work. I liked to keep projections realistic, which was contrary to what everyone else was doing, but I hated setting unrealistic expectations and then simply pressing everyone around me to do more and more and more. It was bad for morale. In my opinion, it was simply not good business.

At six thirty, I left the office.

I arrived at the restaurant quickly enough and left my car in the parking lot they had for personnel in the back. Royal Street was insanely full. Then again, the holiday season in New Orleans was something else. Not quite as crowded as during Mardi Gras, but it was definitely the second-busiest season. LeBlanc & Broussard was filled to the brim, but my brother kept a contingency table in case anyone from the family showed up.

I stepped inside, and the guy behind the welcome desk immediately jumped to his feet. "Mr. LeBlanc, hello."

"Good evening."

"Are you here for dinner?"

"No." The guy's shoulders slumped, relief obvious on his face. "The pralines are being delivered today, right?" I asked.

"Yes. They're already here, in the kitchen."

"Thanks. I'll go directly there."

It would be a madhouse at this hour. But even though I didn't like chaos, I had fond memories of the restaurant's kitchen and the hustle and bustle involved. My grandmothers had put their hearts and souls into this business. As a kid, I was often here with them, and they gave me easy tasks so I couldn't mess up.

When I stepped inside, I took in the scene for a few seconds without announcing my presence. Scarlett, my brother's fiancée, was an excellent chef. Not only had she improved the menu, but the kitchen was running far more smoothly than under the two previous chefs. When I found her, she was talking to Bailey.

What's she doing here? Fucking hell, the woman looked amazing. She was wearing a black dress that was glued to her body. I was going to think about those curves well into the night, I was sure of it.

I took in a deep breath, gathering my wits. *For fuck's sake, Xander, this isn't the first attractive woman you've come across.* But something about Bailey completely disarmed me. Her wavy dark hair begged for my hands to comb through it. I walked toward them with determined strides.

"Xander," Scarlett said, "what a pleasure to see you. I didn't know you were dropping by."

"I heard that pralines were being delivered today."

Scarlett nodded. "Yes. They're so delicious. You should have one."

Bailey gave me a small smile. I tried not to look at her mouth for too long.

She pointed to a small package. "Those are for Celine and Isabeau. Which of you is seeing them first?"

"Probably me," I said.

"Could you give this to them? I made their favorites."

And just like that, I was disarmed again.

"I will," I assured her.

Scarlett looked past my shoulder, then cleared her throat. "Thanks a lot for stopping by, Bailey. I need to get back to the team."

Bailey smiled warmly at her. "Sure. I've heard so many good things about you that when our delivery person got sick today, I jumped at the opportunity to meet you."

Scarlett leaned in, clearly about to say something, but then one of the staff members called her name, and she looked over her shoulder toward the voice. "I'm sorry, I have to go."

"Sure. Don't worry. Let's get out of the kitchen," I suggested to Bailey once Scarlett left, "so we aren't in anyone's way."

"Good thinking," she said.

I guided her out, putting a hand on her back. She leaned into my touch before straightening up and taking a step to the right, as if determined to put more space between us.

I dropped my hand instantly. I didn't want to unnerve her, and it was probably for the best. This was business, plain and simple.

There wasn't much room to stand and talk in the restaurant either. Quite a few people were still waiting to be seated.

"Do you have time to grab a coffee?" I asked her.

She cocked her head in my direction, eyes wide. Why was this so shocking to her?

"Sure, I could do with a hot drink. Although, hot chocolate is my choice of poison at this time of year."

"Right." As we walked out of the restaurant, I added, "There's a good place on Bourbon for hot drinks. It shouldn't be too crazy tonight."

She flashed me a huge smile. "Hey, I'm with a wall of muscle, and it's a weekday, so if not tonight, then when?"

"A wall of muscle?" I parroted.

She narrowed her eyes. "My God, Xander, you have no sense of humor, do you?"

I didn't reply.

"Ha. I stumped you?"

Fucking hell. If this woman knew what was on my mind, she'd run away from me. I had the overwhelming urge to press her against the nearest brick wall and kiss her senseless.

This never happened to me. At least not with someone I barely knew. I was a very cerebral person. I was in charge of my instincts, not the other way around.

But if she kept running her sassy mouth, I *would* end up kissing her.

"I would be careful, Bailey. You're playing with fire." I took a step back because she seemed too perplexed and said, "This way."

For a few seconds, neither of us said anything. Then we moved on.

Bourbon Street was madness, but I'd gotten used to it. I didn't know why it had the reputation for being unsafe. I'd passed it numerous times in my life, and no one ever tried to pick a fight. Then again, as Bailey pointed out, I *was* tall and strong. I wasn't being arrogant, just factual.

"So... how come you couldn't outsource the delivery?"

"Xander... we're grabbing hot chocolate. Could we make small talk or something?"

"Like what?" Small talk had never been my forte. I found it a waste of time. Several dates had no qualms about telling me how much I sucked at it too.

"Like, what do you think about the decorations that we already put up for Christmas?"

I jerked my head back.

"You don't do small talk, do you?" she asked.

"No, not a strength of mine," I admitted. "I get straight to the point."

"Right. Okay."

We continued walking to the bubble tea shop that had opened recently. I came here by accident once, thinking it was a coffee shop. It had all manner of strange drinks, but my niece had wanted to try the hot chocolate.

"Bella had the one with marshmallow, and she swore it was the best thing she ever drank," I told Bailey.

"Who's Bella?" she asked.

"My niece. My brother Chad's daughter. Although, she's a kid, so I'm not sure if her tastes are the same as an adult's."

"Oh, please, I love marshmallows with my hot chocolate." She winked and turned around, looking at the menu scribbled by hand on a chalkboard above the counter.

"What can I get you?" the vendor asked after the couple in front of us left.

"I'll have whatever she does."

Bailey glanced at me before focusing on the vendor. "I'll have a hot chocolate with marshmallows, honey syrup, caramel syrup, and a praline."

My eyes bulged. "Actually, just hot chocolate for me." Her order sounded like an explosion of sugar.

"Coming right up," the vendor said.

Bailey turned to me, and I could tell that she was holding back laughter.

I sighed. "Just say it."

"I knew you were going to change your mind once you heard my order."

"I didn't realize anyone could like so much sugar."

"I make pralines for a living... for now, at least." Her smile was still in place, but the light in her eyes dimmed a bit.

For the first time in my life, I didn't care to talk about business. I wanted to ask more about her. Why had she chosen this line of work? How on earth could she enjoy it so much?

For God's sake, I had to get myself together. The whole reason I came here tonight was to get more insights on the business and why I need to sell it, not learn more about the woman I was potentially about to lay off.

After we grabbed our drinks, we stepped to the side. There was a wooden counter running along the wall.

"Want to stay here and drink it?" I asked.

"Sure."

She took a sip and said, "Holy shit. Bella is right. This is amazing. It's like gooey goodness in more gooey goodness. I can't believe I've never had this in my life." She looked up at me. "Why are you laughing at me?"

I hadn't even realized I was smiling. "I'm not. I like watching you enjoy this."

"Hmm," she said, then took another sip. "Behind those judgy eyes, I can already hear you thinking about how I could be using this time for business purposes. Isn't that right?"

I straightened up. "Not exactly."

"Oh goodness. Let's have at it." She set her cup down on the counter. She had a line of chocolate on her lower lip, and it was all I could do not to lean in. Instead, I glanced down at my cup, steadying myself.

"If some parts of the business were automated, you could certainly use your time better. For instance, if you used more kitchen machines and didn't do individual wrapping of the pralines but rather batched them, that would speed up the process."

I looked up at her. She was blinking rapidly.

"When did you even think about this? How did you even know that I wrap every praline manually?" she asked.

"It's obvious from the layout of the boxes," I said. "And when I came in, you were mixing the batter yourself."

"We do have kitchen appliances," she said, "but some things taste better if done by hand."

"And this whole delivery thing can be easily outsourced," I continued. "That way, you wouldn't run into issues like this when some of your team members get sick."

Bailey took another sip of her hot chocolate, tapping her fingers on the cup. After lowering it, she said quietly, without making eye contact, "Xander, I actually like this way of doing things. I understand that you want this branch to be more profitable, and that's your right, of course. It's your company." She looked up at me. "But there's no need to put down my current process. We get the job done, and customers shower us with praise. We bring people joy."

"I'm sure you do, and I'm not trying to minimize your impact," I assured her. "I sincerely apologize if it's coming across that way. I realize I'm being blunt, but I don't mean to offend you."

She nodded. "I know that. So, what other suggestions do you have for... making the business more to your liking?"

"I haven't thought about it too much. This came to mind by observing you yesterday and today. I'll need more time and information to make an actual plan."

"I see." She took a few more sips and then realized her cup was empty. She started picking out the remaining marshmallows with a small wooden fork.

"Want another hot chocolate?" I asked.

"Oh, no. That would be too much sugar, even for me."

"Look, I'm sure you want more in life than baking sweets. Making pralines can't be your end goal. It's beneath a pastry chef."

I instantly realized my mistake, but it was too late. Her eyes went completely cold.

"Again, I mean no offense, and—"

"I don't know, Xander. That sounds a lot like an insult to me. And not even the best hot chocolate in the world can make up for it."

Turning around, she headed out of the shop without another word.

Which was nothing more than I deserved.

CHAPTER FIVE

XANDER

Mealtimes at the LeBlanc-Broussard household were always a bit crazy. But things escalated to another level entirely during the Christmas season. My parents and grandparents started celebrating almost as soon as Bailey did. There were no carols throughout the house, and they hadn't decorated the place fully, but little bits were popping up everywhere—red candles on the mantelpiece, mistletoe hanging in random spots, and everything smelled like cinnamon.

"All right, everyone," Isabeau said, coming out with a tray of finger foods. "Dinner's going to be a while, so let's all dig in with this. Oh good, Xander, you've arrived. Lovely."

I stood in the doorway. I had no idea how I always managed to be late to family gatherings, but I was starting to accept it as a fact.

"Bella, I have something for you," I called to my niece, who hadn't noticed me yet.

She turned around, and her face exploded in a huge smile. "You brought my favorite hot chocolate."

"Yes, I did."

She ran toward me, snatching the drink from my hands before I could tell her it was hot. But she was a smart girl and held it from the very top of the cup.

"And you put marshmallows in it, too, just the way I like it."

"Of course. I wouldn't dare bring you the wrong order," I told her.

"That's why I love you, Uncle Xander."

I'd never tire of watching this little girl look at me like I'd hung the moon. I had no idea what I did to deserve this kind of affection from her, but I welcomed it.

The entire family was here, sitting on the couches in front of the ancient fireplace, the fire already crackling. It was my favorite part of the house. I lived in a penthouse in a modern building because I liked all the amenities, but I couldn't deny that this home had its charm.

I grabbed a slice of po' boy and immediately inhaled it.

"This is delicious, Isabeau." Since my grandmothers used to be chefs, every single snack they made was out-of-this-world good. My brothers and I had been very spoiled growing up. "And this is for you two." I handed them the box of pralines Bailey gave me.

"Excellent!" Celine exclaimed as I sat down.

Isabeau sat on the empty armchair next to mine. "So, I take it that you met Bailey and Avery?"

"I did."

"What did you think?"

"I'm going to keep an eye on it" was all I replied. I didn't want to get into any details with them.

"Hm," Isabeau said. "That's corporate talk."

"That shit doesn't fly here," Celine said.

I just stared at her as Isabeau laughed. "Oh, Celine, I told you not to try and use kids' language. Sounds ridiculous when you do it."

"I know, right? But I wanted to try it." Celine grinned. "Anyway, let's not nag him. He's got plenty of things on his mind. Besides, we can always ask Avery and Bailey. See what gossip they've got."

"You'd gossip about me?" I inquired.

"Not *you*, specifically. Just this whole situation." Isabeau winked at me, then turned to Celine. "Let's check on dinner."

After the two of them left the room, my brother Julian took the spot Celine had vacated. His girlfriend, Georgie, then sat on his lap. These two were inseparable. I still couldn't believe that he'd actually gotten engaged. He'd been determined for so long that he was a bachelor for life that I'd actually started to believe him.

Georgie kissed the side of his neck and said, "I'm going to let you talk to your brother, okay? Bella said she wants to show me something in the kitchen. Your grandmothers apparently taught her some new trick."

"Sure, babe, you go," he said, his eyes following her as she left the room.

Then he turned to me as Anthony and Beckett joined us too. Our youngest brothers ran the bakeries and music venues and an assortment of other things. They were very good at splitting their focus among the various branches. Unlike them, I was very good at one thing only: numbers. They tended to take everything in stride and always said that being so rigid would be my downfall. I didn't think my way was better than theirs, just that different things worked for different people.

"We need updates. You managed to successfully brush off the grandmothers but not us," Julian said.

"Updates on what?" I asked, confused.

"I can't believe you're obsessing over the confectionery business. It's not even a business," Anthony said.

"That's the problem. I don't like that we've got so many side things going on that don't make money. It's making us lose focus."

Julian cocked a brow. "Dude, the Orleans Conglomerate's been around for decades. A pet project that doesn't make money isn't the end of the world."

"Besides, the pralines are damn good," Beckett chimed in.

"That's beside the point," I said. "And this is where you and I differ. I like the numbers to be as clean as possible. Making a profit makes us all happy."

"You're hopeless," Beckett said. "Why don't you relax a little? Christmas is around the corner. Don't be so tense. Bad for the heart, I heard."

"Dude, seriously," Julian cut in. "Some things aren't supposed to improve. For example, when I realized that my decision to change the supplier for our float's decorations would actually put Georgie's business in danger, I just changed course."

I cocked a brow. "What do you mean? You didn't check all the suppliers and prices to choose the best?"

"Jesus Christ," Beckett muttered.

Anthony just shook his head. "Dude, it's a float. We sponsor it for Mardi Gras."

"You're too much of a control freak for your own good," Julian continued.

"You met Avery and Bailey, right? They do a good job," Anthony said. "I like them."

"Of course they do a good job. I'm not questioning that. And I haven't met Avery, only Bailey. She's doing things she shouldn't even be doing. It's a waste of her time."

Anthony fixated on me. "Why don't you just shut down the operation, then?"

"I promised the grandmothers that I'd leave it running for this Christmas," I instantly replied.

"There's more to it," Anthony said. "You're just not saying it."

"I think a new owner would bring on a different team. I don't want to leave Bailey and her sister out of a job before Christmas," I admitted.

"Aha, he *is* human!" Beckett exclaimed. "You know, I was doubting that for a second. Thought he might be a robot or something."

Anthony stared at me and then threw his head back, laughing so loudly that most of the room turned to look at him.

"What's so funny?" Zachary asked. He was stoking the fire.

"We'll fill you in later," Anthony said before focusing on me.

Beckett pointed a finger in my direction. "You wouldn't usually give a rat's ass about any of this. Am I totally wrong to think that Bailey's gotten under your skin?"

"You're very off base," I told him in a blasé tone. "If I deem it necessary, I will shut down the business."

"Ha! No, I'm not off base. Damn, I didn't expect this."

"I call bullshit," Julian said. "I bet you're not going to shut down anything."

"I need you to fill me in now," Zachary said, joining our group.

"Damn, man. Not one word," I warned the others. "Just nip this in the bud."

"Ha ha, you wish," Beckett interrupted. "That's not how gossip works. And this is just simply too good."

"What's happening?" Zachary asked.

"You know how Xander's newest obsession is the confectionery business?"

Zachary blinked at me. "I wasn't even aware that was an actual business. Don't we give all those pralines away for charity?"

"Well, long story short," Beckett said, "he's mellowing out."

I groaned. "I'm not. And this conversation is getting out of hand."

Zachary looked at the rest of our brothers, then at me. "If you intended to close it, I'm surprised you haven't done it already."

"Yeah, but he likes Bailey far too much," Beckett added.

"Wait, Bailey. Let me think... Oh yeah! She's hot. Both of them are, though," Zachary said.

"Does everyone know the sisters besides me?" I asked.

"Yes," my brothers answered in unison.

"That's because we're always here at the open house event, and you've missed it for the past few years," Zachary explained.

I frowned. "There are too many things happening during the Christmas season. I can't keep up with everything."

"So, what's your plan?" Zachary asked.

"I'll let the business run as it is over the Christmas season and keep an eye on things." Why everyone was making such a big deal out of this was beyond me. There was nothing personal about it. Yes, Bailey was hot, but one thing had nothing to do with the other.

"Meaning Bailey," Beckett said. "Dude, you're obtuse."

"What?" I asked.

"You heard me. You're obtuse."

"I meant keep an eye on the confectionery." I sighed. "You're not going to let me live this down, will you?"

"No chance, and if he does, the rest of us are here to remind you. By the way, thank you for confirming it," Anthony said triumphantly.

I decided not to take the bait and went back to explaining my plan. "In January, after the dust settles, I'll decide. But in the meantime, I'll contact some potential businesses that could be interested in buying off the branch. Just to gauge interest."

"Smart," Anthony replied.

"Why, thank you for the compliment," I told him. "Now, are you all done busting my balls?"

"Hmm," Zachary said, turning to the others. "We're on very thin ice here. If we keep giving him shit, he's going to explode. And that's going to take all the fun out of it."

Zachary always had an uncanny feeling about situations. I liked busting my brothers' balls and could take it in return, but he was on the money with this one.

"Yeah, judging by the look on his face, you're 100 percent right," Anthony said.

Beckett glanced around. "When did everyone disappear? And where?"

"The kitchen, probably," Julian muttered.

"Let's see what they're up to."

"Isabeau and Celine probably finished preparing dinner and everyone has already started eating," I offered.

"Let's go. I wouldn't want you to be left starving," Beckett said.

That had never happened in the LeBlanc-Broussard household, but you never knew with my family. We were all big on food.

As we went to the kitchen, my mind wandered to Bailey again. I knew I was right about the future of the confectionery business, but I'd gone about it all wrong. She was pissed at me—for good reason—and I felt guilty. Besides, this wasn't the right way to conduct business, even if my family owned it. I wanted to make it up to her, and I knew exactly how to do it.

CHAPTER SIX

BAILEY

"'Dashing through the snow,'" I kept singing to myself as I moved around my kitchen. It smelled like mulled wine. I'd even propped up my iPad against the wall and put a video of a fireplace on it.

I truly did need all the coziness possible because I had a ton of work to do. We'd had a mishap at work today. The electricity went out for a couple of hours, which set us back immensely. In retrospect, Avery and I should've just gone home as soon as it happened and continued to bake from there, but I'd hoped the generator would kick in.

Long story short, it hadn't, so I'd still had to take everything home. Now, it was six o'clock in the evening, and I still had enough work to keep me until well past midnight. I had more pralines to bake and package, but I was focusing on the positive—that tomorrow a lot of people were going to be happy to get the pralines on time. I didn't like disappointing anyone.

My mulled wine was more diluted than usual because I needed all my wits about me, but it still put me in a good mood. I took a small break after I shoved the new batch into the oven. I was waiting for the others to cool off enough so I could package them, so I poured myself a cup and moved my hips about as Mariah Carey's "All I Want for Christmas Is You" came on.

My stomach started to rumble. *Whoops.* That didn't go with the chorus at all. I had to order some food, or I was going to start shoveling pralines into my mouth instead.

As I grabbed my phone, I noticed that I had an unread message from a number I didn't recognize.

Unknown number: Hello, Bailey. This is Xander LeBlanc. Listen, I apologize about the way things turned out last time. I'd love to meet up and make it up to you. Let me know when you get this.

Oh, that infuriating man. I was such a pacifist, and yet somehow he managed to make my blood boil. I was tempted to ignore the message, but then I'd spend the rest of the evening thinking about it. That would fill me with a lot of bad vibes, and I strongly believed that my mood affected the way food I made tasted. I wasn't going to spread bad vibes around Christmas, so it was best to get this over with.

I called his number and put the phone to my ear. I was keeping my fingers crossed for Xander not to answer, but he did.

"Hello, Bailey."

"Hi. Sorry, I just saw the message."

"Don't worry. Listen, do you have some time tonight to meet?"

I took a deep breath. "Unfortunately, no. We had some issues at the confectionery today, so I'm behind. Still need to finish some things."

"You're still there?"

"No, I'm at home. The ovens didn't work. I'm elbow deep in making more pralines and packaging the ones we already have... and ordering dinner."

"I can drop by with dinner," Xander said instantly.

"At my house?" I asked incredulously.

"If you don't have anything against it. Do you?"

I didn't know how I felt about having this sexy yet exasperating man here in my house. Then again, perhaps it was better to meet him on my territory. Maybe the good vibes in my house would mellow his grumpy nature.

"Why not?" I gave him my address.

"Perfect. I'll be there in half an hour, maybe forty minutes."

My stomach rumbled again. "Sure." That gave me some time to make up a few more boxes.

After hanging up, I took a look around the kitchen. The place was a mess. Granted, my whole house was in a bit of a disarray these days. I called it the "Christmas mayhem look." Since I was running around the whole time from

November until January, I didn't have time to keep things picked up. I wasn't a slob by any means, but I wasn't a minimalist either. I filled my place with all sorts of things.

My home was cottage core and yet very modern. It was on the same property of a large, gorgeous house. The owners had built this place as an Airbnb at first, then quickly realized it was far too much work. They couldn't dedicate so much time to it, so now they were renting it out permanently. I had huge floor-to-ceiling windows overlooking the small yard. They'd even planted shrubs around the bungalow so they could shield it from the view of their house. I was truly super lucky. It was off the beaten path, and I drove forty minutes to the confectionery every day, but I wouldn't change it for the world.

I checked on a batch of pralines I'd pulled out nearly two hours ago. It was cold, so I started packing them carefully and managed to fill up three boxes. Almost unwillingly, Xander's words came to mind.

"If you... didn't do individual wrapping of the pralines but rather batched them, that would speed up the process."

He was right, of course, but I thought it added to the specialness of the treat every time you unwrapped a praline.

When my doorbell rang, I startled in my chair. Had forty minutes already passed? I checked the clock and, yep, indeed they had.

I rose from my seat, wiping my hands on a kitchen towel before hurrying to the front and unlocking the door. When I pulled it open, I let out a mighty sigh. Xander LeBlanc might be a huge grump, but he was certainly very nice to look at. He was wearing a suit and nothing else. True, the weather was pleasant today, but couldn't he have put on a jacket or something anyway to hide all that sex appeal? I bet he wasn't even aware of how hot he was.

Nah, he probably was.

"Good evening, Bailey."

I sniffed the aroma coming from the bag he carried. "Hi. It smells delicious, like..."

"Shrimp and chicken jambalaya," he said with an actual grin—the first I'd ever seen on him. It only added to his good looks, damn it.

"That's my favorite. Thank you."

"I know. I called my grandmothers after talking to you and asked them what your favorite food is."

I nearly did a double take as he stepped inside and I closed the door. "Wait, what?" *Who is this man? Where's grumpy Xander?*

"After the way things ended last time, I couldn't show my face around here with food you don't like, could I?" His grin was still in place.

Was it possible that this major grump actually had a sense of humor and maybe even a heart?

I didn't want to jump to conclusions too fast. He was simply trying to get into my good graces for some reason.

But why would he? He owned the company. If he wanted to close it, he could do so tomorrow, and I had no say in it. It was his prerogative.

"Thanks. That was very considerate of you."

"I'd have brought you hot chocolate, too, but from my experience, it's no good if it's cold."

"Define your experience," I said, taking the bags with the food and leading him to the kitchen.

"Once, when I went to spend some time with Bella, back when my brother was still single, I bought her hot chocolate. Not from the place on Bourbon, though. It wasn't around back then. Anyway, the dang drink was cold by the time I got to their house, and I discovered that microwaving it somehow ruins it."

Oh, man. I was melting, and I absolutely didn't want to. I truly needed my wits about me when this man was close to me. He'd bought hot chocolate for his niece. And he'd brought my favorite food. He couldn't really be that bad, could he? There had to be some soul in him if he was related to Celine and Isabeau, even if they didn't share the same views on the confectionery.

Once in the kitchen, I quickly realized that there was no place to eat. When I turned to Xander, he was looking around with wide eyes.

"What happened here?"

"Told you, I'm working."

He looked in the oven, too, then at the new batter I'd whipped up and the boxes on the counter. "Bailey," he said, "this will keep you up half the night."

"I know."

"Why didn't you tell me?" he asked. "I could've dropped by another evening."

Hmm, decisions, decisions. Should I be totally honest with him?

Well, why the hell not? He's been more than blunt with me.

"I wanted to get this over with."

He trained his gaze on me. Oh, those eyes. They were my kryptonite, I swear. I quickly looked away.

"Get this over with?" he parroted slowly.

"I figured that if I postponed this, I'd keep thinking about it the whole evening. Then I'd package all the pralines with bad vibes."

If I thought his eyes were wide before, it was nothing compared to now. They were almost comical. Why did they have to be so vibrant green? It was my favorite color too.

"Good to know where I stand," he said, then schooled his features.

I felt sassy again. "Was that too honest?"

"Sort of. A lot of people think it, they just don't say it to my face."

I laughed. "Oh, Xander, you can always count on me to say the exact same thing to your face and behind your back." That was not strictly true, though, I realized. I'd also told Avery he was hot as hell, and I'd never tell him that.

"Let's go to the living room. There's no point trying to make space here."

"How can I help?" he asked.

"You can grab two plates from that cabinet." I pointed above the sink.

He took out the plates, and I immediately put the jambalaya on both of them. "You chose the same?"

"Yeah." He moved closer to me, taking a knife from the dish rack.

That smile he gave me was downright seductive. I couldn't figure this man out. Why did he want to get on my good side? It literally made no sense.

He didn't have any need for it. And yet if there was something I understood about him, it was that he didn't waste his energy doing things that were unnecessary.

But it didn't matter. I was having my favorite dinner, and hopefully after he left, I could focus on my pralines again.

He grabbed both plates, and I walked in front of him to the living room, where I had a small round table with two chairs. The only company I usually had was my sister; I didn't invite friends over, as it was too small for that, and I liked being out and about in the city when I did socialize, especially the French Quarter.

"Your house is very welcoming."

I looked over my shoulder before we sat down. "Are you trying to butter me up?"

"Yes."

"It's a bit messy right now, but the Christmas season is far too busy for me to focus on anything else. You haven't commented on my Christmas carols." The music was still playing in the background.

"It's just the way you are."

"That's right!" I dove into my jambalaya, shoveling a few mouthfuls in before stopping for a breather. God, I was so hungry.

I closed my eyes, sitting back in my chair. *This is just what I needed.*

Xander

"This is one of the best jambalayas I've eaten," Bailey said.

I could barely take my eyes off her. Her hair was sticking to her temples, and her skin was flushed from working in the kitchen. She looked exhausted but still beautiful. I couldn't stop drinking her in.

"I won't say it's the best, but let's not start an argument already." I winked at her.

Two seconds later, she asked, "Where's your favorite from?"

"The one Isabeau makes," I replied without hesitation. "She's got a special recipe, and I've yet to eat one that's better."

"She did actually offer to bring me some jambalaya once. I turned it down, figuring it's too much work. But if she offers, again, I'll take her up on it."

"Trust me, it's very good."

She laughed. "I'll remember that."

She ate so quickly, it made me think she might have skipped lunch.

"Bailey," I said carefully, "when are these boxes you're working on due?"

"Tomorrow," she answered before shoveling in another mouthful.

"Fucking hell. That's going to take a lot of work before you're done."

She nodded. "I know. Which is why I'm happy that you brought jambalaya and livened up this evening a bit."

"I'm starting to get compliments?" I remarked. "That means we're making progress."

She tilted her head, narrowing her eyes as if considering her next words. "I'm still on the fence about that. Let's see how the rest of the dinner goes. So far, you showed up in a relatively good mood and with my favorite food. You're off to a very good start."

I started to laugh. My entire body relaxed in her presence, which was something I wasn't used to. When it came to business, I always had my guard up. My mind was on numbers and strategies; I didn't laugh or joke around. It was my MO.

But this wasn't about business anymore. I had to be honest with myself—it was about Bailey.

"I have a proposition," I said as we were both on the last few spoonfuls of jambalaya. "I'll stay and help."

She frowned. "Help with what? It's just two dishes. I can put them in the dishwasher."

"With the boxes and the pralines."

She looked at me incredulously and then waved her hand. "It's fine. I'm good on my own."

"Bailey, you're going to get tired, you know that. How many boxes do you have to fill?"

She averted her gaze. "Quite a few."

"And you've got another batch that needs to be baked. And you have to wait for it to cool off too. I saw the batter, so you can't deny it."

She'd opened her mouth as I was speaking, likely to do just that, but then closed it and just nodded.

"We'll be faster between the two of us," I encouraged. There was something drawing me to her, and I wanted to spend a bit of time in her presence to see what it was. Maybe as we got to working, I'd realize it was nothing—but I doubted it.

She narrowed her eyes again, and I knew I was about to get some more attitude. I fucking loved it. I could do this with her all night. Actually, I could do so much more than that. Her mouth was—

No, I was *not* going to start obsessing over it again.

"Really? You've got experience baking pralines?" she asked.

"No," I admitted. "But I'm good at following instructions."

Now she was the one who started to laugh. She moved her legs under the table, and they crashed into mine.

"Oh, I'm so sorry," she said between guffaws.

"Don't worry about it."

That slight touch only prompted me to want more. I almost reached for her over the table, but to what end? I truly wasn't myself when I was around Bailey. I was the stick-in-the-mud brother—I owned up to that with no shame. I was focused on numbers and was cutthroat when it came to business. My feelings were secondary and had been suppressed for so long, I wondered if they might be dead. But right now, trying to keep my guard up around this woman was exhausting.

"You know what? I want to see this," she said with an impish smile. She had a dimple at one corner of her mouth. We were definitely off to a good start.

After we finished our food, we moved back to the kitchen. Somehow the place seemed even worse now than when I first saw it. I was starting to register the details: the number of boxes, the stack of packaging for each praline, the trays set around the room to cool off the candies. But then I noticed something on her stove.

"What's that?"

"Mulled wine. Honestly, not my best pot. I only put in a smidge of actual wine. It's mostly just cranberry juice. Want to try it?"

I wrinkled my nose. "No, thanks. You didn't exactly sell me on it."

"That's okay. I had two cups and don't need more, but I'll keep it simmering because I like the smell."

"It does make everything more festive." I clapped my hands together. "All right, put me to work. What am I starting with?"

"Packaging. That's the only thing I can truly trust you with. Let's do a box together. It's not rocket science, but it's better if you see the way I do it."

"Sure." I liked her attention to detail. She approached things the way I would.

We both sat down at the wooden table side by side, and the impulse to touch her grew even stronger.

She pulled an empty box in front of us and said, "This is one of my favorites. I love our Christmas editions."

"It looks exquisite," I remarked. Someone receiving these treats would feel special and well thought of, unlike giving a gift of candies from the local drugstore.

"I chose the red velvet," she said, caressing the cover with her thumb. "It feels like you're holding a Santa Claus costume, you know?"

I actually didn't know, and in my mind, it all seemed a bit far-fetched to me. But she was speaking with so much enthusiasm that I absolutely didn't plan to ruin it.

That was probably the reason why I was the brother in charge of the numbers. I was the first to admit that my people skills were nothing to brag about.

"All right, so each praline goes into this plastic cover, and then we wrap it with the red ribbon."

I couldn't believe it. Even the ribbons had to be hand-tied. *For fuck's sake.*

"I always make a double knot," she continued.

I laughed. "Want to make people work for it?"

"Sort of. I think if you do, it tastes even better, keeps it fresh longer. And you don't run the risk of eating the whole box at once."

That *was* good thinking. But also, it was very expensive for an employee to be wrapping these one by one when a machine could do hundreds in no time at all.

Of course, that would be if we were *keeping* the confectionery, which we weren't.

"Now you do it," she said.

I tried to follow her steps, but my ribbon looked decisively shittier than hers. "That looks amateurish. But with enough practice—"

"You're going to make half the pralines look bad," she finished for me.

"Something like that." I didn't like feeling inept or out of my league, but this was clearly not my strong suit.

"Why don't you put all the pralines in their individual bags, and I'll do the ribbons?"

"No, let's do this. Tying the bows is the most time-consuming. Let's practice a few more times. I'll get the hang of it. I'm a quick learner, I promise." I was not going to give up.

She looked at me dubiously, and I wanted to kiss that snarky smile off her mouth. I was used to people doing exactly what I wanted, when I wanted, without question. But having this sassy woman challenge me was a breath of fresh air that I didn't seem to mind. And coming from Bailey, it was exactly what I needed.

"Sure. Let's try again."

I watched her do another one and then carefully replicated her moves. By the fourth one, they'd started to look decent.

"Will you look at that?" She leaned in so close that I could smell her perfume. "You really are a fast learner."

"Have a little faith in me, will you, Bailey?" I teased.

She straightened up, the tip of her nose so close to me that I could barely keep myself from tilting in even more, closing the distance, and kissing her. Like it was beyond my control.

Pulling back, she said, "If you continue like this, I just might. I'll keep a close eye on you, though, as I move about the kitchen, and if you fall too far behind, I'll come over to help."

I winked. "Of course. I wouldn't have it any other way."

"Do you mind if I leave the Christmas carols on?"

I looked into her eyes. "Bailey, this is your home. You can do whatever you want. Just act as if I'm not even here."

"Ha, I can't. If you weren't here, I'd probably toss my bra." She immediately pressed a hand to her mouth, her eyes wide.

Fuck, I had to get that image out of my mind, but it was impossible. Her body had kept me up at night anyway. Bailey was petite, but she didn't lack curves. Quite the opposite, actually.

And now I couldn't help but imagine how she'd look without a bra on, how her nipples would poke through her shirt. I could feel my control slipping away.

Bailey jumped from her seat. "Um, okay, let's get to work."

"You really have your hands full during the Christmas season."

She smiled. "Honestly, it's not that bad. Back when I worked in software, every day was highly stressful."

I stared at her. "Wait, what? You worked in software?"

"You should know that. I'm not even a pastry chef at all. Your grandmothers never told you?"

"No. I always assumed... Never mind."

"I met Isabeau when I was on a burnout vacation from work. I wanted to occupy my time with something, so I took up making desserts and pralines. She convinced me to work at the confectionery."

I was stunned. She'd actually *chosen* this life. I felt like an idiot. Why had I not even bothered to ask how she'd come to do this?

"Your financials must have taken a big hit."

"Of course you'd go there." She smiled, and I rightly felt chagrined. "Avery and I also have a side business. We teach people how to make sweets in an amateur online academy kind of thing. It's been surprisingly profitable, even in the age of free videos on YouTube, so money is good. Although, probably in the long term, if the confectionery closes down, I'll either have to look for something else in software or..." She shuddered. "You know what? Forget I even said that. It's never going to be an option. My sister and I will expand our business."

"This is completely unexpected," I admitted.

"Why? Couldn't you see me working in a corporate environment?"

"Honestly, no. I assumed this is what you've been doing forever."

"No. Ever since I was small, I worked hard toward being a software developer. I was good at it. Somehow, I thought that if you're good at something, you're supposed to do that. But it ended up being a soul-consuming job. And now that I know the alternative, no way in hell would I go back to working in corporate. No offense."

"I don't feel insulted at all. This is very interesting."

"I also took off because my father had been sick for a while, and I was literally working twelve hours a day from Monday to Friday. On weekends, I barely had time to do anything other than sleep, let alone help my parents."

"Is he okay now?"

"Yes. He's made a full recovery. But he couldn't keep up with work, so he retired. Mom is still working." She hesitated a moment, and I noticed her eyes were a little glassy. "So anyway, now you know why the confectionery is so important to me."

I felt her words like a punch to the gut.

"But I didn't want to make you feel even more guilty." She winked at me. "So, let's focus on the boxes."

Fortunately, I was so bad at wrapping the pralines that I actually *had* to focus on it. It had the pleasant side effect of taking my mind off Bailey. And as the evening went on, I realized something else.

"Working with my hands is actually relaxing," I told her after we'd sealed two boxes.

"I know, right? It's partly why I love this so much. And I happen to think that some of that energy goes into the pralines."

That was a little too woo-woo for me, but she was so adorable that I didn't contradict her.

"Why did you put separate batches into the same boxes?" I asked her. "Did you intend to mix them up?"

"Yes. Each box has a different selection of pralines."

"Huh. I didn't even realize until now. They all look the same from the outside."

"Yes, that's the point." She was sitting next to me again, and her face completely lit up. "That way, people will never know what they're going to get. I mix and match all the boxes. No two are the same. It's a mix of cherries and pears, mint and banana. I try to keep track of all the favorites. They keep changing, which makes this so much more fun. Never a dull Christmas season. Isabeau and Celine actually mentioned mint and banana. I made a batch for myself and loved it."

Her entire body had transformed in the past few seconds. She seemed open and relaxed and simply happy right now. Part of me was starting to understand the appeal of doing everything by yourself—it kept you from getting bored.

It was midnight by the time we finished. I couldn't believe that she'd wanted to do this all alone. She probably would've been here until at least three o'clock.

"Xander, thanks a lot for staying with me. You really didn't have to."

"My pleasure."

Was it my imagination, or was she blushing? Was her mind going to the gutter as often as mine?

As she walked me to the door, she swayed a bit. Probably from exhaustion, if I had to guess.

"Can you take the day off tomorrow?" I asked her.

"Why would I do that after we managed to pack up everything?"

"You're bone-tired, Bailey. You should rest."

"I'll rest after the season's over." She looked down at her feet. "Hopefully not permanently."

"Bailey—"

She looked up. "I don't want to start this conversation. You said we're fine for this Christmas season, and I'll focus on that. I will *not* have any Grinch energy in this house."

I started to laugh. "Where exactly are you delivering all this tomorrow?"

"To your grandparents' house, actually."

"How come?"

"They take part in the open house tour on Christmas."

"That's true." It was a big event in New Orleans.

"I've done the house tour, like, three times because it's lovely. You were never there. I would've remembered."

"Why? Because I'm such a Grinch?" I tilted my head. "Or have I impressed you in some way, Bailey? To make myself so memorable?"

Looking away, she licked her lips. "You LeBlancs are memorable," she said far too quickly, which could mean that she was hiding something.

I wanted to outright ask what she meant, but I didn't want to put her on the spot. Not right now. I'd have plenty of opportunities.

"I'll be there this year," I decided on the spot.

She whipped her head up to face me again, eyes wide. "Wh-Why?" she stammered.

"Because, as you correctly pointed out, I've missed it far too often. It's a pity, don't you think? Besides, I want to see how people react to the pralines after everything you've told me tonight." *And you'll be there.*

Her shoulders sagged a bit. "Oh, so that's part of your observation strategy."

"That's right." The truth was, I was simply longing to see her again, and this seemed like the perfect excuse. Being around Bailey and my family at the same time might be tricky—they were giving me enough grief about her as it was—but I could handle them.

"Then I guess I'll see you tomorrow, Xander."

"See you then."

After I stepped out of the house and she closed the door, I took in a deep breath. *Mission accomplished.* Unfortunately, I was more attracted to her now than before I'd stepped foot inside the house. I had no idea how, but this woman was growing on me despite her obsession with Christmas carols and good vibes.

I wanted to call Isabeau on the way to the car, then realized it was far too late, so I just went home instead. However, I called her first thing the next morning.

"Hey," she greeted.

"Hi, Isabeau."

"To what do I owe this pleasure?"

"I always like to check in."

"True, but you're always busier this time of year finalizing books. Or at least that's what you tell us."

That earned her a chuckle. I adored my grandparents, and Isabeau might be my favorite.

"I have a surprise for you. I'm going to drop by the open house event this evening."

"Goodness. Are you serious?"

"Yes, I am." I could hear the joy in her voice, and I suddenly felt like I'd neglected my family. Was I focusing too much on work?

"Oh, wonderful! Is this Bailey's doing? Did she convince you?"

That caught me off guard. "Why would you say that?"

"Because we've never been able to get you away from your office."

I cleared my throat. "I want to see how people react to the pralines she's bringing and so on."

"Uh-huh. Is that so?" I could practically hear her smiling.

"By the way, I wanted to ask you for a favor."

"Sure."

"Could you make your famous jambalaya? I dropped by her place last night with some jambalaya, and it was nowhere near as good as yours." I realized my mistake immediately, but there was no taking it back.

"Why exactly did you go to Bailey's?" she asked in a stern tone.

I quickly explained about their production issues earlier in the day, skirting around the *why* I went there in the first place. Isabeau didn't need to know that I wanted to get back in Bailey's good graces. That would kick-start another round of questions altogether that I didn't even have answers for.

"Of course I'll make jambalaya." Her tone was completely different now, softer. "What time are you stopping by?"

"I don't even know. When does it start?"

"Oh, very early, about three o'clock."

"Do people not work in this town?"

"Oh, Xander. Yes, they do. But this is... You know what? It doesn't matter. Just come whenever you can."

"When does Bailey usually arrive?"

"Five."

"I'll try to make it in time."

CHAPTER SEVEN

BAILEY

Open houses were some of my favorite events. I took pralines to six of them, all in the Garden District. But the celebration at the LeBlanc-Broussard mansion was truly the best. I arrived at five o'clock on the dot. Adele and her husband, Remy, were always doing the tours. Usually, both sets of grandparents—David and Isabeau, Felix and Celine—stayed in the enormous living room, chatting up guests.

I was carrying the praline boxes in two huge baskets. They were heavy, but I was used to it. I considered it my arm workout.

David opened the door and led me to the living room. I was smiling for no reason as I took in the decorations. They were always magnificent. In the past, they had four Christmas trees throughout the house, which some might think was over the top, but for a Christmas lover like me, it was heaven on earth. Red ribbons and garlands with gold and red clips were spread around everywhere. They'd reached a perfect balance while still making it very cozy.

"Bailey, darling. Excellent, you're here. Is it just you this year?" Isabeau inquired.

"Yes. We ran into some issues with production yesterday, so my sister had to stay and manage a few other things."

"Xander told me."

"He didn't give you grief, I hope?" Celine asked, coming to Isabeau's side. The guests she'd been chatting with turned to the buffet.

I shook my head. "Not at all. If he hadn't helped me wrap and pack, I would've probably worked until early in the morning."

Celine's mouth hung open.

Isabeau tilted forward. "Did we hear you right, my dear? Xander, our grandson? He helped you pack boxes?"

"Yes. And wrap and tie each individual praline."

"Honey, that doesn't sound like Xander at all. Are you sure?"

I started to laugh. These two were unbelievable.

"You're a good influence on him... if you can put up with him." Celine sounded perplexed.

"The way I see it, I've got nothing to lose. So, where should I put the pralines? The usual spot?"

They both nodded, so I put them down at the very edge of the table near the dessert section.

"Would you like to tour the house?" Isabeau offered. "The next one starts in about fifteen minutes."

"I think I'll just stay around here, thank you. Anyone else from the family coming?" I asked in a careful tone.

"Most of the boys. And of course Bella with Scarlett, baby Simone and Chad. And Xander said he'll be here this year." The look on Celine's face made me think she didn't believe he'd show.

I tried not to look too surprised. "Oh, that's good. This shouldn't be missed. I feel like the house tour is the official start of the Christmas season."

"Oh, so many of our guests say the same. That's why we choose to do it so early before everyone else starts their celebrations," Celine mentioned.

Isabeau grinned, throwing a suspicious glance at Celine. These two always looked like they were up to no good, but even more so today. "Besides, Xander requested that I make my special jambalaya for you."

And now my cheeks were red. "Oh my God, I'm so sorry."

"What in God's name are you sorry about, girl?"

"That he put you to work."

Isabeau scoffed. "First, no one can make me do anything. I do what I please. And second of all, I've always wanted you to taste my jambalaya."

He called his grandmother? Aww, here I was, melting again. God, why couldn't I just be immune to the man?

Xander was a phenomenon. He could be so stoic and inflexible in his thinking when it came to business and profits, but then he'd ask his family to do something for me. He was a challenge that I was beginning to like.

"I made a huge portion of jambalaya," she continued.

"All on your own?"

"I wouldn't dare interfere with her recipe," Celine said. "We each have our specialty."

"I'm so excited to taste it, but I'll wait for everyone else to arrive."

"I think most of them are here," Celine said just as there was a chorus of voices from the corridor. I recognized Xander's among them.

Every cell in my body was on fire. Goodness, I hadn't even seen the man and was already in this state. Last night had been confusing, but that was probably because I was overwhelmed, and it was just the two of us in my tiny, tiny space. His sex appeal seemed to take up all the air. I was certain it wasn't going to be the same here, though. This house was huge, and by the sound of it, there were a lot of LeBlancs out there in the foyer.

They filtered in one by one, and I noticed Xander immediately. He zeroed in on me, and my mouth instantly went dry. I pressed my thighs together on instinct. The tips of my nipples felt white-hot too.

Nope, I was wrong. This was absolutely going to be just like last night.

He was holding the hand of a girl who seemed to be no older than ten. That had to be the famous Bella. I tried to rack my brain, but I didn't remember her from past years. Then again, there were always kids milling around at this event, so maybe I'd simply missed her.

Scarlett came straight to me. She was holding an adorable baby in one arm. "Bailey, it's so good to see you. The pralines are a hit! I stole one for myself, too, of course. It made my evening."

"Thanks, that means a lot to me." Coming from a chef, it was high praise indeed.

"Hey, Bailey," one of the LeBlancs said. I thought it might be Beckett, but I couldn't remember. "I'm Beckett," he added, clearly reading the confusion on my face.

I smile sheepishly. "Sorry, I get the names mixed up."

"No wonder," Xander said, "with so many of us."

My body reacted to his voice quite differently than it had to Beckett's. My heart went pitter-patter, my underwear felt strangely warm, and my tongue stuck to the roof of my mouth. I was a goner.

"Hey," I replied.

"So, you know everyone?" he asked.

"I don't think we've met," one of the men said. "I'm Zachary."

I shook hands with him. What was it with the genes in this family? Did they all have to be so hot?

"I *think* I know everyone else... at least visually."

"Well, then, let us introduce ourselves again. I'm Anthony," the guy next to Zachary said.

He went on to tell me everyone's name, though I was pretty certain I'd forget them soon enough. I had half a mind to just call them "sexy guy one," "sexy guy two," and so on. They certainly deserved the nickname.

Isabeau cleared her throat. "Feel free to jump to the buffet. The guests will be coming and going, looking at the house. I don't think you'll see your parents much this evening."

"I can help with the tour," Zachary said.

"That's lovely of you," Isabeau said. "They'll probably be here in about five minutes, and you can ask them. Anyway, I've made my special jambalaya," she added, looking directly at Xander. To his credit, he kept a straight face.

There was a chorus of "Yes!" from around the room. I wasn't the only one excited about this.

"Uncle Xander, can we go put the star on the fourth tree?" Bella asked him.

He was still looking at Isabeau but said, "Sure, let's go. The star is by the tree?"

"Yes, I laid everything out," Celine said.

I watched Xander and Bella go to the nearest tree.

"It's their tradition. They do this together every year," Celine whispered to me. "But they usually do it on Christmas Day."

He had traditions with his niece? And I'd thought I couldn't melt any further. Boy, was I wrong.

Xander lifted Bella after she grabbed the star. He held her up high, enough so that she could put the ornament right in the middle of the tree—it wasn't a tree topper after all.

Cold and calculated people didn't hang out with their family and have traditions with their niece, right? Maybe there was hope for him to let the confectionery stay up and running after all.

After he put Bella down, he turned around and zeroed in on me once more. I suddenly felt as if we were alone in my small house again. The power this man had over me was scary.

He walked toward me with determined strides. When he was within earshot, he whispered, "Try the jambalaya."

"Did you really tell Isabeau to make it for me?"

Xander glanced down for a split second. *Holy shit. He was looking at my mouth.* I was suddenly super jittery, as if a current of electricity had gone through me.

"I did." He made eye contact again.

"Why?" I whispered.

"Because I knew you'd enjoy it. Go on, try it."

Give him a sassy reply. Don't lose your wits. "Still trying to get into my good graces?"

He leaned in closer. "Maybe I have another ulterior motive in mind."

It was on the tip of my tongue to ask if he wanted to get into my pants, but even I knew that was far too much. It bordered on unprofessional. And Xander was the ultimate professional... until now.

"Can you give me a hint about what the motive is?" I straightened up again so we could make eye contact.

"No. I can't even believe it myself, let alone admit it out loud."

I sucked in a breath. Wait, what did that mean?

"Come on. I'm curious to hear what you've got to say about the jambalaya."

Was he serious? Why would he change the subject? He couldn't drop that on me and not tell me what it meant. Was he attracted to me, or was I somehow misreading this entire situation? Last night, I'd thought that I'd made things up in my mind because... well, he was a sexy guy, and we'd been far too close.

Xander led me to the buffet, putting a hand on my arm. At the contact, I swear I heard him suck in a deep breath. I looked at him as surreptitiously as possible. He was breathing deeply, as if he was concentrating on something.

I couldn't believe this guy was single. He was *so* good-looking.

Wait a second. I didn't actually know if he was single. I instantly felt chilled to the bone. *Oh shit, I hope I'm not fantasizing about someone else's man.* Even though I hadn't made a move, it still felt wrong. It was on the tip of my tongue to ask, but it truly was none of my business.

At the buffet, I went straight for the jambalaya. I didn't even really care about the rest.

Scarlett was right next to me. "I love Isabeau's jambalaya. I can't make one that even comes close to it."

"Now I'm even more curious to try it. So, how come you moved to New Orleans?" I asked her.

"I wasn't happy with things in Seattle anymore, and I needed the change. Plus, I was obsessed with New Orleans as a kid. And as an adult, it didn't go away," Scarlett said. She was a beautiful woman, and very kind too. I'd liked her from the first time I saw her when I made the delivery at the restaurant.

"It actually continued when I started watching *The Originals*."

I instantly grinned. "You're a vampire girl?"

She nodded with a wide smile. "Through and through."

"So am I. Though I only watched *The Vampire Diaries*. *The Originals* being filmed here sort of felt spooky and too close to home."

I'd heard great things about the spinoff, though, and maybe at some point I would watch it.

"I'm a Damon Salvatore fan," I told her.

She wiggled her eyebrows. "Klaus Mikaelson girl here."

"What's going on?" Xander asked. "Who are Damon and Klaus?"

"These superhot guys," I explained.

Xander looked at us with a frown, especially at Scarlett.

"Yeah, they're superhot," she agreed.

"What?" he barked.

"Pity they're fictional, though." I managed to keep a straight face, but Scarlett burst out laughing.

I gave Xander a short explanation about the TV show. "Ha ha, very funny," he deadpanned once I'd finished.

"Oh, it was. You should've seen your expression." He'd seemed... almost jealous. I initially assumed he was upset because Scarlett was his brother's fiancée, but what if there was more to it?

Come on, find out if the guy is taken and put your mind at ease.

An idea popped into my head. "So, out of everyone, just you and Chad are a couple, right?" I asked Scarlett.

She gave me a knowing smile. "Julian also has a fiancée, Georgie. She's adorable, but they couldn't make it tonight. The other guys aren't taken."

I gave her a noncommittal shrug and then proceeded to fill my plate with jambalaya. I could tell just by looking at it that it was superior to anything I'd had before. Filling a spoon, I brought it to my nose to smell. The texture was richer, but the flavors were familiar.

I shoved the spoonful into my mouth before stepping aside to make space for others, and oh my God, I was in heaven. I closed my eyes, focusing on the taste. This wasn't just the best jambalaya, it was the best food I'd ever had. It was creamy but not heavy. The mix of shrimp and meat was simply amazing.

I opened my eyes, which was when I noticed Xander watching me with a smile. I'd thought he was still at the buffet. When had he come up to me? I seemed to be aware of him no matter where he was in the room, but apparently the jambalaya had required all my attention.

"I take it, it's to your liking."

"Yes! I have to figure out the recipe."

He scoffed. "Good luck with that. She won't even show it to family."

"This is the highlight of the evening."

"No, the eggnog is."

"There's eggnog?" I asked.

"There will be soon. That's actually my specialty, so I have to make it fast," he replied.

I was so surprised that I nearly dropped my plate. "What? You, Mr. Grinch, know how to make eggnog?"

Xander tilted closer. "What do I have to do to get you to stop calling me that?" he whispered in a low, seductive voice.

Whoa!

"I wouldn't even know where to begin. It's, like, a whole list."

"Well, while you're working on that list, why don't you come to the kitchen and watch me make it? Maybe that's going to change your mind about me. Unless I'm keeping you from doing a tour of the house or something."

"I've already had a few of those in the past. But... I didn't intend to linger too long tonight."

"Trust me, my eggnog is worth the wait."

"Hmm, I feel like you're trying to oversell it."

He tilted even closer. My goodness, if he kept doing so, I was going to simply jump his bones and kiss him.

My own thoughts scared me. I might be full of sass, but I was the worst when it came to making a move. I'd never had thoughts like this before, but now they were running amok.

"All the more reason to stay. Please." His voice was teasing, but somehow his pleading seemed sincere.

"Of course. I don't actually have anything else planned. This was the last delivery for today. I guess I can just enjoy the rest of the evening."

"Perfect!"

I looked at my plate. "I want to take some more jambalaya before going to the kitchen. I'm afraid it might be gone otherwise."

He winked at me. Wait, was that a butterfly in my stomach?

I dashed to the table again. More than half of the jambalaya was already gone. Clearly it was a favorite in the LeBlanc household. I smiled as I filled my plate for the second time. I felt just a little bit guilty that I wasn't leaving much for the guests, but what the hell. This was my chance to eat it, and I wasn't going to forsake it.

Xander was still waiting for me in the same spot when I returned. His eyes seemed a bit darker than when I left him. At first, I thought it was maybe a trick of the light, but then I realized he was looking me up and down. I was wearing a simple sweaterdress, but the man was staring at me as if I were wearing some sort of super-sexy mini. This one wasn't even that fitted to my body.

"I actually forgot where the kitchen is."

He snapped his gaze up, blinking slowly as if he was clearing away confusion. "I'll show you."

Chapter Eight
Bailey

The second I stepped into the kitchen, I smiled. Like every other room in this house, it was large, with a huge island in the middle. Then again, with two chefs in the house, this was no surprise.

"Someone already prepared everything for me," he noted.

We went directly to the stove.

"So, your specialty, huh?" I questioned.

"I've been on eggnog duty ever since I was sixteen."

"Duty?" I laughed.

"Yeah, we each contribute as much as we can to the same old traditions. I have to say, I'm the least involved of all. I usually do this for our traditional Christmas get-together, but since I'm here today, I wanted to do it."

"I like your traditions. Putting up the star with Bella, prepping eggnog."

I looked at the ingredients on the counter: egg yolks and sugar, milk and whipped cream, nutmeg, vanilla extract, and cinnamon.

"We have all the right ingredients except one. No alcohol?" I asked him.

"Nah. Once we tried to make one for adults only and a separate one for Bella, and it backfired because she kept wanting to taste ours. Let's just say she wasn't happy when we didn't let her. Ever since, we just drink alcohol-free eggnog."

"Fine by me. So, put me to work," I said.

He stared at me. "No! You worked enough yesterday. Now you just relax."

"But I made *you* work yesterday too."

"You needed the help. Besides, I can whip this up in no time."

To my astonishment, he didn't even need to consult the recipe. I was watching him with my mouth slightly open. Seeing this mountain of a man at the stove made him even sexier, especially when he took off his suit jacket and rolled up his sleeves.

Sexy forearms. Of course. Why couldn't he have super-thin nonmuscular forearms?

Because they wouldn't go with the rest of his body, you dummy, a voice said in the back of my mind.

"Bailey?"

"Hm?"

"Where did you go just now?"

I shrugged, trying to play it cool, but I knew I was failing because his smile just widened. "I don't know. Why? Did you ask me something?"

"I asked if you've got any tips for an eggnog recipe."

"I don't often make one, but that might change after tonight. You've got to give me your recipe. Actually, wait. I'll taste it first and then see if I want your recipe or not."

"You still don't trust me, huh?" he asked as he poured the nutmeg into a bowl.

"I require proof."

"You're more like me than you think."

"Meaning?"

He laughed. "It was a compliment."

I grimaced. "Sorry, I didn't mean to imply that it wasn't. I do look up to you in many ways."

I was focusing on his hands for no reason at all.

"You have skills in the kitchen," I commented.

"Yeah, I told you that yesterday when you wouldn't let me near the stove."

"I figured—"

"That there was no use?"

"I wouldn't put it quite like that." *Goodness, I need to watch myself with him.*

"But close. I grew up with two chefs as grandmothers. There was no escaping cooking in my family. With so many of us, we kind of took turns with it."

"I assumed your grandmothers wanted to be in charge."

"Nah, they worked a lot during that time. Mom cooked often, but we kids gave her a hard time."

He glanced at me, and yep, that really was mischief in his eyes. "We kept teasing her that her food was no match for that of the grannies'."

"Poor Adele. It must have broken her heart."

"Not really. She openly admits that she doesn't like cooking." After the pot started simmering, he said, "It's gonna need half an hour."

"Wait a second, we can't drink this tonight. Doesn't it need to cool off in the fridge?"

"No, we always skip that part."

"Wow. Now I *have* to taste it. I never thought you could skip such an important step."

He chuckled. "We wing it very often in my family. If something tastes good, it doesn't matter how you prepare it. That's our motto. Well, that's the motto of everyone else except the grandmothers. But then again, the rest of us are just lowly mortals, not chefs."

There was nothing left for him to do for now, so he turned sideways, training his eyes on me.

"I'm glad I came tonight," he said.

"I'm glad too. It was really nice to see you with your family."

He looked at me for a few seconds before saying, "I love my family, but I came tonight to see you."

I gasped lightly but managed to disguise it as a small cough. "Me? You wanted to see me? Why?"

I was standing with my back at the kitchen island, and Xander stepped in front of me. "Because I enjoyed your company a lot last night, and I didn't get enough. Not nearly enough."

"Xander," I murmured, "I know you're trying to be on good terms, but really, this is your company and—"

"Fuck the company. This is not about that."

My pulse quickened, and my breath caught. "What is it about?"

He was very close, and there was heat in his eyes—there was no mistaking it. But I had to hear it from him. I couldn't believe it otherwise.

"It's about you. Just you." Then he touched my cheek with the back of his fingers. "You've been on my mind constantly ever since we met."

"I gave you such a hard time. That doesn't make sense."

"That was precisely why I couldn't stop thinking about you."

Now he was close enough that his hot breath brushed my skin. Heat gathered between my thighs, and I pushed my legs together.

"Xander. Last night—"

"I wanted to kiss you at every turn."

I pushed my hips forward in a knee-jerk reaction and pressed myself right into him. That's how close he was.

He groaned and kissed me in the next second. His mouth was hot and so full of passion. It demanded the same from me, and I gladly gave in to the kiss. God, I didn't even know I needed it so badly.

His hand moved from my cheek into my hair, wrapping it tightly, then bringing me even closer to him. I felt his other hand on my back and then sliding to my hip before finally moving under my ass. I was lost to this man. So lost, in fact, that I didn't even realize what was going on until he lifted me off the floor and put my ass on the counter.

He was pressing my thighs to his sides, and since he was touching me so freely, I did the same. I moved my hands on his shoulders and then down his chest. Goodness, the muscles on this man seemed unreal. They were perfectly formed and so hard that I couldn't get enough. I needed skin-on-skin contact. I needed everything. No one had ever stoked such a fire inside me or made me lose my head that way.

The sound of someone clearing their throat made me come back to my senses. My lips felt cold as Xander took a step back, looking straight at the door.

Oh my God, someone caught us kissing!

My face felt like it was burning. I was so flushed that I thought I might faint any second now. I didn't even dare turn around.

"We need you in the living room." It was a guy's voice, but with my back turned, I couldn't tell who it belonged to. At least it wasn't Isabeau or Celine, but it had to be someone from the family.

"We'll be right there," Xander said.

How did he look so annoyingly calm and composed? The man wasn't even blushing. I felt like a roasted tomato.

When the footsteps faded, he turned his gaze on me. His eyes were super dark and even sexier than before. "I'm sorry."

"Oh." My smile fell, and I quickly hopped down from the counter. "Umm... we can pretend it didn't happen." I pulled my dress down to my knees and smoothed out the nonexistent wrinkles just to give myself something to do.

Xander touched my arm, and a current of awareness moved through me. I instantly straightened up. He gripped my chin next. "I didn't mean the kiss. I'm not fucking sorry about the kiss, just that we were so rudely interrupted. I had big plans."

There was the man I knew, straight and to the point.

"Really? What were they?" I was suddenly feeling a little better about our getting caught.

"Something completely impractical for the kitchen."

Holy shit! My nipples turned to tight buds; they were almost painful against my bra.

"I completely forgot we were in the kitchen." Xander seemed to revert back to his sensible self, and I had to smile.

"Funny, I totally forgot that I was in your grandparents' house too."

He looked at the eggnog. "This is ready to put through the strainer," he said. With dexterity, he grabbed the utensil and the simmering pot and poured the contents into the empty pot right next to it.

"My God, you're strong," I whispered.

"What was that?"

I laughed nervously. "Nothing, I was talking to myself."

After putting down the pot, Xander turned to me. "Bailey, we just passed that stage where you have to keep your dirty thoughts to yourself."

"Who said I had dirty thoughts?" Ha! If he only knew.

"I can read your body language. Right before the kiss, you pressed your thighs together." His voice was suddenly an octave lower.

"Yes."

"Was it because you were wet?"

I got even wetter at his words. I couldn't say it, so I simply nodded.

He closed his eyes, taking a deep breath. "Fuck," he murmured. "We need to join the others."

My heart was beating out of my chest. What was I doing, kissing this man, flirting with him? I was working at the branch he planned to close. This thing was messy anyway. Why was I making it even worse?

But when he fixed his gaze on me, I couldn't think straight.

"Or what?" I murmured.

"Or I'll lose my head completely."

I needed to tease him more than I needed my next breath.

"What would that entail?" I prodded.

He swallowed hard. "Closing the kitchen door, turning the lock, and taking you right here on this counter. And next to it and on the floor and on that chair. And every other place there is."

I could barely breathe past the tension gathering in my body. How did we go from zero to dirty talking in no time at all? I didn't have time to mull it over too much, though, because someone joined us again.

"You can have another kissing session once the guests are gone. Come on, let's go." It was the same voice as before. It belonged to Beckett, who winked at me before leaving.

I covered my face with my hands and groaned. "I can't show my face out there. What will your family think?"

Xander caressed the back of my head, then kissed the top of it. The gesture warmed me in a different way altogether. It was sweet, and that wasn't a word I thought I'd associate with this man.

"Don't worry about Beckett. He won't say anything to the family or put you on the spot. He'll give me a hard time, but not in front of anyone else. You can trust me on that."

"Maybe we should go separately, so it's not too obvious, I guess?"

Xander looked at me with an expression I couldn't read. "Sure, if that makes you feel better. Go ahead. You can tell everyone I'm still checking on the eggnog."

"That sounds like a good idea." I quickly made my way around the island.

When I reached the doorway, Xander said, "Bailey?"

"Yes?" I looked over my shoulder.

"This conversation we started here isn't over."

And just like that, my pulse was out of control once again, but I gave him a smile. I hadn't thought it was either.

"By the way, I need that recipe. I wasn't paying attention to anything other than your forearms."

He laughed wholeheartedly. "I'll go one better. Whenever you want to make some, I'll come to your place, and we'll make it together."

Chapter Nine
Xander

"If no one has anything else to add, I'll adjourn this meeting," I said. My brothers were all in the meeting room of my office building to discuss next year's budget.

Beckett put his hands on his head, interlacing his fingers. "I don't have any questions, but just so we know, are you hurrying to get somewhere?" he asked, smirking.

"I've got no more updates. And there's no shortage of work that needs to get done." I knew where he was going with this, but I wasn't going to tell him a thing.

"Dude, can you relax a bit? It's almost December," Chad said. "Take it easy. I thought it was a good sign that you stopped by the mansion for the house tour, but you're still as uptight as usual."

"It wasn't for us," Beckett said. "He had an ulterior motive."

What had gotten into him? Last night, I'd lectured him back at the house to keep his mouth shut, and he had.

"He was just showing off for Bailey," Anthony jumped in helpfully.

Chad cocked a brow. "Why?"

"I want to be on good terms with her and her sister. I don't like creating unnecessary conflict while we're deciding next steps," I explained.

"Xander, you want to close down the confectionery. It's an open conflict no matter what you do," Chad said.

"I'm managing it."

"But this is the funny thing, though," Zachary said. "Why *are* you 'managing it'? I still can't figure that out. You usually don't care about what others think. I'd understand if you put in the effort to achieve an amicable relationship with a company you're trying to acquire, but this is different. You must really like her."

Beckett's smirk grew even more pronounced. They were starting to ride my ass too much. It was one thing to harass each other when we met privately, but we were on the clock. No time to waste.

"I've got my plans. And when the time is right, I'm going to share them with all of you. There's no need to guess."

"We wouldn't want that," Julian replied, fighting laughter.

"All right, let's not keep our brother from the rest of his afternoon," Chad said. "He's probably got a few more meetings lined up."

That was usually true, but not today.

Once they left the meeting room, I went straight to my desk in my office and opened my laptop, checking my calendar once again. I'd had a very specific reason for asking my assistant to free up my evening—the Celebration in the Oaks was today, and from the spreadsheet Bailey had sent me a while ago, she was going to be there at 6:00 p.m. on the dot, which was in forty minutes. I had plenty of time to make it.

I started to laugh at myself. This wasn't like me. I was always decisive. When I wanted something, I went for it—and I wanted Bailey so damn badly.

Last night, I'd wanted to be alone with her again, but it had been impossible, as my grandmothers monopolized her. Then Bella wanted my advice on how to deal with a girl at school who was giving her trouble, and I gave her all my attention. I never wanted her to feel like she was an afterthought, because she was one of the most important people in my life. So I'd gone with her to the dining room, and we'd sat down until we made a plan. When I returned to the group, Isabeau said Bailey had already left.

I'd wanted to take her home and talk about what had happened. Kissing her like that was just more proof that I was completely different around

Bailey. All my instincts worked on a different frequency than usual, and I had no power over them. Frankly, it was exhilarating.

I'd stayed far too late yesterday with the family to call her after I left. And when I woke up this morning, I decided that instead of calling, I'd just show up at the Celebration in the Oaks. The light show was huge, though, so I had to figure out exactly where she was. There was a note that said "Mr. Bingle," and I ventured to guess that meant she'd be there handing out pralines, but I wanted to make sure. However, I didn't want to call Bailey; I wanted to surprise her.

As I went to my car, I got an idea. I asked Lydia to send me Avery's phone number. She did so even before I'd climbed into the driver's seat, and I called Avery right away. Fortunately, she answered quickly.

"Hello?" She was breathless.

"Hi, Avery. This is Xander LeBlanc."

"Hi, Xander!"

"Listen, a while ago, your sister sent me the schedule of where the pralines are going to be delivered. Is she the one going to the Celebration in the Oaks tonight?"

"Yes. It's one of her favorite events," Avery said.

"Where's the drop-off point, exactly?"

"You know where Mr. Bingle is?"

"I'll figure it out," I said.

"She'll be there in about twenty minutes, I think."

"Thank you."

"You're heading that way?" she asked in a strange voice.

"Yes."

"But you saw her last night."

Fuck. Why didn't I prepare for this? I'd actually met Avery a few times and knew she had an inquisitive nature. "I did." Had Bailey told her about our kiss?

"Is there anything I can help you with?"

"I'd like to discuss some things with her."

"Listen, I'll be super honest, Xander. My sister said you've been dropping by a lot. She's already feeling a lot of pressure regarding this whole thing with the confectionery. I know you're the boss and everything, but I'd appreciate it if you would take it easy on her."

I started the car, getting ready to leave after I hung up. "Avery, I assure you, I'm not putting any pressure on her."

"Then why do you keep meeting up with her? You can lay it on me too. We know it won't be good news."

From her perspective, my meeting up with Bailey obviously looked bad. She was just being protective of her sister.

"No offense, Avery, but what I want to talk about is between Bailey and me. It's personal."

"Oh," she said. "*Ohhhhh.*" And from that one word, I deduced that she'd put two and two together. "You're... Okay. Um, wow. Sure. Um, never mind. Forget everything I just said. Wow. That would explain why my sister was... Never mind. Right. *Soooo*, I guess have fun, then. She does like to stay for a long time at the celebration. And just so you know, she loves all those light shows. She sees them every year."

"Thanks for the tip."

"You're welcome." She still sounded stunned.

I hung up and left the parking lot, hoping to get there somewhat quickly, so long as I didn't hit much traffic. It could be hit or miss when it came to the holiday season, especially with all the various festivities happening all throughout the city.

As I approached the destination, I realized I had to actually look up exactly where the famous snowman was. It had been years since I'd been to the Celebration in the Oaks. The last time I'd come was when Bella was three years old. She'd been fascinated by it. The light show spanned a few miles, as far as I could remember.

I found a map easily enough, and I had time to inspect it when I ran into traffic. Once I arrived, I parked quickly, to my surprise.

After getting out of the car, I headed to the snowman, determined not to be too late. I didn't want to miss Bailey.

There were vendors selling all sorts of snacks and drinks. The air smelled like cinnamon. Even though the Christmas season was always a rush for me, I had to admit that the atmosphere here was very festive. It reminded me of my childhood.

Out of the corner of my eye, I saw a stand selling hot chocolate. Checking the time, I noted that I still had a few minutes left, so I went straight to the vendor. It was an elderly woman wearing a woolen cap and what seemed like five layers of clothes.

"Hot chocolate with marshmallows, please."

She looked me up and down and said, "I wouldn't expect someone who looks like you to order this kind of drink."

My eyes bulged. *Did she really just say that?* "It's not for me."

"Oh, for the missus. Good choice," she said, winking at me.

Missus! The word sat strange in my mind. I didn't correct her, though. I simply wanted to get the drink and find Bailey, not waste time making small talk.

Since I didn't engage her, she didn't add anything else. Besides, a line was forming behind me. By the time I paid and took the cup from her, there were already five people waiting. Now, I only had to find Bailey.

I watched the crowd around the huge snowman, scanning everyone. Then I saw her. She looked so damn adorable. It was a cold evening—far too cold for New Orleans. She had a cap on and... mittens, maybe? It definitely looked like it.

She was chatting with a woman and was holding a dozen individual holiday bags. The other woman took them from Bailey as I approached. By the time I was close enough to hear what they were saying, Bailey noticed me. At first, she narrowed her eyes, but then they went completely wide as her mouth formed an *O*. She zeroed in on the hot chocolate a moment later, and her face instantly exploded into a smile. She probably noticed the marshmallows too. They were floating on top.

"Xander, what are you doing here?" She turned to her friend. "This is Xander LeBlanc. He's the owner of the confectionery."

"Mr. LeBlanc. What an honor!" She shook my free hand. "I'm Jasmine. It's my first time actually meeting a LeBlanc. Thanks a lot for sending us all these pralines every year. They're always a highlight with the kids."

I smiled at her, schooling my features so it didn't look like I had no idea what she was talking about. What kids did she mean?

"I made some extra this time because last year there were quite a few from a group home"—Bailey's voice faltered a bit—"and we didn't have enough for everyone."

"Don't beat yourself up. You did make an extra batch and had it delivered to them the next day. I'm sure everyone got one," Jasmine told her.

"I know, but they were so disappointed!"

Wow. How could she care so much that she was still upset about it a year later?

"This is for you," I said, handing her the hot chocolate.

She couldn't hide her grin any longer, letting it take over her face as she accepted the drink.

Jasmine looked at the marshmallows and then at Bailey, clearly putting two and two together. "I'm going to leave the two of you. Enjoy the rest of the celebration."

"Do you need my help at the stand?" Bailey asked her.

Jasmine shook her head. "No. The team is here this year. We're on top of it."

"And you'll let me know in case anyone is without pralines?"

"Will do," Jasmine said, then waved to us both and walked down the sidewalk.

The second we were alone, Bailey took a sip of the hot chocolate. "This is so good. Where did you get it from? I didn't see a vendor."

"Not far from here. I'll buy you another one later on if you want."

She looked up at me, eyes narrowed. "You're trying to earn points again?"

"I just want to keep you happy," I said without thinking. The admission took me by surprise, too, but it was 100 percent true.

"How did you even...? Oh, I sent you that spreadsheet."

"Yes, I did. And it's proving even more useful than I thought. I called Avery, too, just to make sure I had the right place."

She grimaced. "Huh. So, what exactly did my sister say?"

"She lectured me first about showing up everywhere... and then I think she got the right idea."

"She's going to give me an earful tomorrow." She took another sip of hot chocolate, then pulled her beanie even lower on her ears.

"Why is that?" I asked, instantly feeling protective of her.

"Because she's my older sister, so it's her prerogative." Glancing at her feet, she murmured, "Why are you here, Xander?"

"Because we've got some unfinished business from last night."

Chapter Ten
Xander

"Oh, I thought... Never mind." She quickly brought the cup to her lips.

"What did you think?"

She shook her head more vehemently as she looked up. "It really doesn't matter."

"It fucking does. Tell me what's weighing on your mind."

"Since we didn't get to talk any more, I assumed that you want us to forget about it."

I leaned in so damn close that I was completely in her personal space, but after last night, I needed the closeness. And she wasn't pulling away—quite the contrary.

"Are you kidding me? All I wanted last night was to find another minute alone with you. I wanted to take you home and—"

She looked up abruptly. "Oh my God, you did?"

I could practically feel her body relaxing.

"Don't tell me that you spent the entire night thinking I was some kind of asshole who avoided you on purpose."

"I don't know. Maybe not on purpose. But it did cross my mind."

"No, I just... got distracted with Bella."

She smiled. "I saw you. It was endearing."

"And then I wanted to talk to you, but you were gone by the time I rejoined the group."

"It felt like I was intruding once the guests left."

"You were not intruding," I said, touching her cheeks with my fingers. I was dying to taste her lips again.

"Do you mind moving out of the way? We want to take pictures with Mr. Bingle too," a guy said.

I looked right at him, preparing to tell him to mind his own business, but he was with his wife and three kids. So instead, I took Bailey's free hand and pulled her out of the way until we were quite a distance from Mr. Bingle.

"Do you have time to talk now?" I asked.

"Can we walk and talk?"

"Sure. What do you want to do?"

"We can walk through Carousel Park."

"Walk, not drive?" I double-checked.

"It's just two and a half miles."

"Precisely, and then we have to come back to the car."

I took in her pink cheeks, the way she kept moving from one foot to the other. Despite the hot chocolate, she wasn't warm. Moving was a good idea.

"You do the walk every year?" I asked her.

"Of course. Don't you?"

"I haven't done it in years."

She gasped. "No way. You don't come to see the lights? But they're so beautiful. For me, they symbolize everything that's good about Christmas."

"You can be my guide."

"With pleasure."

"You want another hot chocolate?" I offered.

She hesitated. "No, there aren't too many toilets on the way." Then she dropped her head back and sighed in desperation. "Ah, why did I tell you that? I'm not really good at making a sexy impression."

I laughed. "Bailey, it's an important, natural observation. Besides, you're so damn sexy that I'm having a really tough time staying here with you."

"As opposed to what?"

"Going in a dark corner, preferably somewhere warm, and finishing what we started last night."

"Xander," she murmured. "God, the things you say. I wouldn't have penned you for a dirty talker, what with your suits and cuff links."

"I have far more surprises in store," I assured her. Even though it was dark and the light only shone on half her face, I knew she was turning red.

"Let's get moving," she said, "because I'm really starting to get cold. Should've worn my UGG boots."

"What's that?" I asked her.

"Ah, some boots with a lot of fur on them. I actually think it's fake fur. Doesn't even matter. They keep me warm, but they're not really a thing around here because it doesn't get that cold, does it?"

"Except for tonight."

"This way," she said, pointing to an alley, and I followed her lead. Even though many were headed here tonight, it wasn't overly crowded.

"I wonder if Jasmine needs any help. We could go by the stand."

"No," I said firmly. "We are not going anywhere near there."

"Why?" She eyed me suspiciously.

"I'm sure you'd jump to help them whether they needed it or not."

She shrugged. "Guilty as charged, but I know how these things are. You're always like 'Oh, we have a big team,' but then it turns out that there's a huge line or something."

"Bailey, you work long hours. You need to rest a bit from time to time."

"Not during the Christmas season, I don't. That's the busiest time. I look forward to it all year. Isn't it the same for you?"

"It is busy, but not in a good way."

"Is that why you haven't been here in so many years?" she asked.

"Something like that."

"Please tell me you don't forsake all New Orleans traditions, or I'll stop liking you right here, right now."

I brought my mouth to her ear. "I sincerely doubt that. I'm certain I can make you like me again in a matter of seconds." I was close enough to hear her sharp inhale.

"You don't mince words, huh?"

"Not with you." Straightening up, I added, "I actually do go caroling in Jackson Square with the entire family."

Her eyes widened. "You participate in that? It really is one of my favorite things to do. I'm so happy that New Orleans keeps up these traditions. We're so lucky to live in this city. Not many really do stuff like this anymore. At least not as much as we do."

"It's good for tourists."

She looked exasperated. "Oh, Xander, it's like we're from different planets."

That made me laugh. "I'm a practical man."

"Yes, I got that. Don't you do anything at all that isn't practical or useful?"

"I go fishing with my grandfathers from time to time, mostly because they need some adult supervision."

The surprise on Bailey's face was vivid.

"I love hanging out with them. They have a lot of wisdom to impart, and I like to listen to them. And the bayou is a perfect place to recharge. I used to go fishing with them when I was a kid, too, and with Dad as well. He seemed to notice that we wanted time alone with our grandparents, so he often stays home. I've learned a lot from them during our fishing days. I think they instilled in me this love I have for legacy as well."

"You always knew that you wanted to be involved with the Orleans Conglomerate?"

"Yes. There was never any doubt about it."

"And the same goes for all your brothers?" she asked.

"Yes—at least I think so. None of us ever even wanted to work anywhere else."

"I wonder what that must feel like. To know exactly what you want to do. I mean, I thought I did too. That's why I became a software developer. But things turned out differently. Working at the confectionery is the happiest I've ever been."

"Bailey...," I started.

She shook her head. "No. This evening, we're strolling and admiring the lights. We're not talking about anything unpleasant."

I nodded. "Fair enough."

"The Cajun display is one of my favorites. The Night before Christmas," she murmured. "I love the attention to detail."

The wooden house was simple enough, but all the illuminated figurines around it were quite a work of art. They worked well together.

"Want me to take a picture of you with it?" I offered.

"Oh no, I have a million. Do you want me to take a picture of *you*?"

"Not necessary."

"Hmm." She narrowed her eyes.

"What's on your mind?"

"I'm just trying to piece things together about you, and I'm getting a very confusing picture."

I chuckled. "I wish I could clarify it for you, but I'm not my usual self with you."

She tilted her head but didn't say anything else.

She was even more attractive than usual with her beanie, mittens, and red cheeks. They made her green eyes pop even more. Her dark hair was sticking out in all directions from under the beanie. I wanted to kiss the living daylights out of her right there and then, so I stepped closer and then stopped.

"Xander."

"Hmm?"

Her voice was uneven. "If we aren't taking pictures, we should move out of the way before someone yells at us again."

"I keep forgetting we're in public when I'm this close to you," I admitted, and she licked her lips. That did nothing to soothe my need for her, but we did move along.

After another fifteen minutes of walking, Bailey started to shiver for real.

"Damn it. It really is too cold," she said.

"How about we head back to our cars?" I suggested.

She pouted but nodded. "Good idea. I don't want to catch a cold during the busy season. You just never know with the weather."

She raised her hands to the sky in desperation, dropping them back when others started to look. "Last year I was wearing a short-sleeve sweater. That was fine. Did you park in the lot closest to the snowman?"

"Yes."

"So did I."

"I'll give you my jacket."

"No way. I'm not even sure how you're not freezing, but don't take it off."

"I can use my arms to keep you warm." I wiggled my eyebrows.

"I won't say no to that."

That's when I realized she really had to be cold. We quickened our pace, and I rubbed a palm on her back in quick moves, then repeated the motion down her arms.

When we reached the parking lot, we headed straight to her car.

"Who needs more layers when I've got a hot-as-hell LeBlanc next to me?"

I growled. "You keep saying that and I'll kiss you right here in this alley-way for everyone to see."

"Xander, there are kids around here."

"One of the reasons why I haven't done it yet."

She tilted her head sideways. "What's the other reason?"

I stopped walking, and so did she. "Last night, everything happened in a rush. I completely lost control of myself. I should've taken more time with you." This was the gist of what had been on my mind since that moment in the kitchen.

"Well," she said, "it was honestly one of the hottest... Never mind."

"Tell me," I said.

"It's just that... we're in a complicated situation." She folded her arms over her chest but looked up at me. "You need to make a decision about you know what."

"One thing doesn't have to do with the other," I assured her.

"It would feel strange for me. Besides, we're so different. You know, you're a Grinch, I'm not. You can't deny that."

I smiled despite the fact that she'd shot me down. I fucking liked this woman, but what she was saying made sense. And I always did what made sense.

"I'm not."

"So yeah, that's what I think," she said. "I'm not sure this is a great idea."

I looked at her intently for a few seconds, then nodded and stepped aside, opening her car door. "Then there's nothing left for me to do than wish you a great evening."

Her shoulders dropped as if she was disappointed. I sure was, but I didn't say anything else. She told me how she felt about it, and I wasn't going to pressure her.

"You too."

Chapter Eleven

Bailey

Avery was at the confectionery before me the next morning, but that was no surprise. I was running late.

"Morning!" I greeted her when I rushed in. "Mind if I turn on the carols?"

"Not at all."

She was cleaning up the kitchen area. We'd left a bit of mess last night, but we'd both been too exhausted to clean up.

"I'll put on my gloves and join you soon," I promised.

"Thanks. I don't feel good working when the kitchen isn't—"

"Squeaky clean," I finished for her. "I know."

I immediately put on rubber gloves and pulled my hair up in a ponytail. Then I got down to business, spraying every counter and surface. We weren't doing a deep clean, but I didn't want to do a half-ass job either.

"How come you're late today?" she asked.

"Umm... I had trouble sleeping last night." I'd tossed and turned and tossed and turned for what felt like forever. The image of Xander with my car door open kept dancing in front of my eyes, teasing me. Clearly the man had been about to devour me. Why had I turned him down when my entire body was yearning for him?

My explanations felt silly, almost like an afterthought. I'd been tempted so many times to grab my phone and text him, but I knew that was ridiculous. Who would text anyone in the middle of the night?

That's the code for booty call, a voice said at the back of my mind.

"Did you do anything in particular?" She sounded like she was on the prowl.

I glanced over my shoulder, but she had her back to me, scrubbing the wooden table.

"No."

"So, you went straight home after celebration?"

"Yep. It was freezing. I didn't even manage to complete the whole walk."

My sister straightened up, turning to me. "Really?"

"What's up with you today?" I turned around, putting my hands on my hips. "You're acting funny."

"No reason," she replied. But there was for sure a reason. She had a twinkle in her eye. It reminded me of when we were kids and she caught me with my hand in the cookie jar.

"Tell me what's going on," I said, faking that I had no idea.

"I'm just wondering when you're going to fess up."

"About what?" I asked, deciding to tease her.

Her jaw dropped before she laid into me. "I can't believe you. Xander said that he was joining you. And I talked to Jasmine last night. She said Xander showed up with hot chocolate with marshmallows." She said it in a tone that indicated it was all the proof she needed to make her point—which it kind of was.

"Jasmine just told you all of this?" That caught me off guard.

"Of course not. It took some convincing on my part, but eventually I loosened her tongue."

"When did you even do that?"

"Last night, of course."

I shook my head. "Oh, man. What's she going to think?"

"I don't think she knew what was happening. But don't distract me. So, you went home with Xander?"

I nearly jumped back into the counter. "N-No," I stammered. "Why would you think that?"

She frowned. "You really just didn't complete your walk because you were cold?"

"Yes."

"I don't get it," she said.

"First of all, please don't call Jasmine. Just ask me whatever you want to know."

"But you aren't telling me anything!" She was clearly fighting laughter. "Obviously something happened between you and Xander when you went to the LeBlanc-Broussard mansion, and yet I didn't hear a whisper of it except 'It was a very nice evening.'"

I glanced down at my feet and then back at my sister. "We had a lot of work yesterday."

"Bailey! Who can I call to find out what happened at that house?"

"No one," I said even though Beckett came to mind.

"Don't worry. I wasn't going to call anyone. Goodness, I do have *some* decency."

I sighed. "Fine. We kissed at the mansion, and it was very hot."

"How did that even happen? I thought you didn't like the guy."

"I didn't in the beginning. But after he showed up at my house and helped me bag the pralines, I figured that he wasn't a bad person. He just has a different perspective on things."

She raised a brow. "Is he a good kisser?"

I nodded but decided not to share any more details with her.

Now she was grinning. "So, why didn't you continue that last night? Don't tell me he brushed you off. Although, he showed up with hot chocolate," she said, clearly talking to herself more than me, "so that's not possible."

"I just don't think it's smart," I confessed.

My sister let out a breath of relief and closed her eyes. "Thank goodness you're saying that."

"Why?"

"Because I was thinking the same thing. But it's been a while since you've had any action, and I didn't want to take the wind out of your sails."

My stomach bottomed out. "So, you think it's a bad idea, huh?"

"His family owns this place, and I know he wants to shut us down." Her tone was gentle but firm.

"I know that. But he *is* a good kisser," I countered.

"I wouldn't totally condemn you if you threw all caution to the wind. Men have forgotten how to kiss these days. I'm not sure what happened." She looked at me tenderly and added, "But he's treating you nicely, isn't he? What with the marshmallows and helping you at the house?"

"Yes, he is. I think we've misjudged him. He's kind to his family, and he's really cute with his niece. At the house, they spoke for more than an hour, and he was really paying attention. Most people just brush kids off."

"Oh, sister, you really like him."

"How is that a surprise?" I said, turning around and continuing to wipe the counter. "I wouldn't kiss someone I didn't."

"This isn't just a lapse of judgment, like 'Oh, here's this hot guy. Let's test his kissing skills.' You genuinely like Xander."

I didn't reply, not really knowing how, and Avery said, "I admire you."

"For what?" I looked over my shoulder again, then returned to cleaning because she was too busy scrubbing a table.

"Basically turning him down. I couldn't have done that. But out of the two of us, you've always been the stronger one. And you have a good head on your shoulders."

Yes, I did, but where had that gotten me? And why did I suddenly want to be reckless and "throw caution to the wind," as Avery put it? What had Xander told me, that he acted differently with me? Well, it seemed that the same was true in reverse.

"By the way," Avery said. "Maybe we should start making a plan for expanding our online courses. In case this ends up being closed down or sold."

"We should," I agreed. "I already have some ideas."

"So do I."

Extending our online business would be an exciting endeavor. But I wasn't ready to let go of the confectionery. It had become my safe haven.

After we finished cleaning, I cranked up the carols a little bit more. I also put a pot of mulled wine to simmer on the stove, which I planned to do every day from now until Christmas—obviously no alcohol. I mixed all the ingredients for the batter, tapping my foot to the rhythm of "Jingle Bells." I had a playlist with about fifty Christmas songs, but I got excited every time one of the classics came on. They were just a vibe.

I checked the time on my phone and found an unread message. I knew it was from Xander before I even opened the app—I simply felt it—and I was right.

Xander: Morning. Someone brought hot chocolate for all the employees at the office, and it made me think of you. How was your evening? I hope you didn't catch a cold.

I loved that he was checking in on me.

Bailey: I'm good. No signs of a cold. I'm just super tired because I couldn't sleep.

Xander: What a coincidence. Neither could I. I kept thinking of a certain feisty woman enjoying the lights as if she was seeing them for the first time. Why didn't you sleep?

I licked my lips, looking over my shoulder at my sister.

Bailey: I was thinking of a certain grump who doesn't have time to watch the lights at all.

That was a good comeback.

He responded only seconds later.

Xander: He did come to watch them with you. You've got a strange power over him.

My pulse quickened as I shifted my weight from one leg to the other. God, I wanted to hear his voice. I wanted to ask him exactly what kind of power and how far it went, but instead I simply replied to the message.

Bailey: Sounds dangerous.

Xander: It is. Very much so. Do you have a lot to do today?

Bailey: No rest for the wicked. I've still got plenty of deliveries, and a hot handsome man is keeping me away from my work.

What are you doing, Bailey? You told him that this isn't a good idea, yet you're sending him mixed signals.

Xander: Wouldn't dream of it. Have a great day.

I'd essentially told him to leave me alone, yet for the rest of the day, I kept checking for messages. I *so* wanted to hear from this man. Mixed signals or not, I was glued to my phone. But he didn't write anything.

I had to focus on my pralines. They weren't going to bake themselves, and I didn't want to make Avery shoulder more than her share of the work. It simply wasn't fair.

Later in the afternoon, I did get a text from him.

Xander: How was your day? What are you doing this evening?

Bailey: It was productive. I'll relax with a vampire show. You?

Xander: I'm on a date.

I stared at the phone. *What the hell?* Why would he even write that to me? I was about to swear off men, but then he sent me a picture of himself and Bella, and I just melted. My heart seemed to quickly fall back in place again.

Xander: I'm taking my niece out for some beignets. I promised her back at the party, and I can't break my word.

I read his text a few times, smiling more and more. Okay, it was true that he was a grump, but he was also an amazing person. Two things could be true at once, right?

Xander: I wish you were here with us.

Ha. I actually wasn't a beignet person, which was weird for someone living in New Orleans. But I didn't want to say that right now because I was still busy swooning. So I replied with something entirely different.

Bailey: I wish that too.

Way to send a guy mixed signals after turning him down last night. I had no idea where I'd gotten the willpower to do that, but it was melting away completely.

Bailey: Have fun with Bella. I don't want to hijack your time with her.

Xander: That means you're willing to hijack it another time? Let's pin down exactly when.

I started to laugh. Leave it to Xander to try and nail this down.

My entire body was on high alert. *Oh, Bailey, what are you doing?* I had no idea, but I simply didn't have it in me to shut him down again. I didn't want to.

Bailey: You focus on Bella. We'll see about the rest.

Xander: Hell yes, we will.

Chapter Twelve
Xander

"And then we baked another pecan pie. I'm even better than I was at the baking competition at school," Bella exclaimed proudly. She'd chosen baking in the talent competition, and because she and Scarlett practiced thoroughly, she'd won. But my niece was a lot like me—she liked to be the very best at whatever she did. It was no wonder that she kept practicing even after the competition was over.

"Good for you. And pecan pie is still your favorite, huh?" I asked her.

She nodded vehemently. Bella had powdered sugar all over her mouth, chin, and even her cheeks. She'd always eaten beignets like this, literally with her whole face. "Yes, but beignets do come in a very close second. Or maybe they're first and pecan pie is second," she said, frowning at the beignet as if it was a hard decision. "But I want to try other pies as well, like apple pie. Maybe even cherry."

"You want to become a baker?"

"No. I just like spending time with Scarlett. I like how she explains everything, and she never gets mad at me like Mommy."

All right, I'd been mistaken. I thought she wanted to perfect her skills even more, but it turned out that she did it simply because it was an activity she enjoyed doing with Scarlett.

"Your dad says you haven't been to your mom's in a while," I said carefully.

No one in the family truly liked Sarah. We'd all given her a fair shot in the beginning, and I personally didn't have anything against her. Only after my brother Chad revealed that she'd been cheating did I completely change my opinion about her. That opinion only worsened when she started to show less and less interest in her daughter. But we all had an unspoken agreement to never badmouth her in front of Bella. I was simply trying to gauge if my impression from what Chad was relaying to the family was the right one.

"Mom travels a lot these days."

I would never understand how the woman had so little desire to see her own flesh and blood.

"But I don't care," she continued. "I like staying home on weekends. Scarlett has lots of time because she doesn't work brunch, so we do a lot together. We even started reading Harry Potter to my sister. Dad always pretends that he's got work to do when we go to the reading room."

I burst out laughing. "Yes, he told me that."

"But we caught on to him. It's okay, though. I like being with Scarlett. She's really nice to me. I wonder if she'd like to be my mommy officially."

I nearly dropped my beignet. This was a very delicate topic. I cleared my throat. "You would like that," I stated more than asked.

"Yes, she's amazing. And I don't think Mommy would mind." She didn't seem upset about it.

"Have you spoken to your dad about it?" I asked.

"No." She looked at me with big eyes. Putting down her beignet, she laced her fingers together in front of her. I immediately realized she was trying to copy Isabeau. She had the same serious expression too. Though with her face still covered with powdered sugar, it was hard for me not to laugh, but I was doing my best.

"Do you think that's a good idea, Uncle Xander? Tell me the truth. You don't pull punches." Sometimes she spoke like a miniature adult, and it was hard to believe she was only ten.

"I think your dad would be happy to hear what you've got to say, and I'm sure Scarlett would too."

"But what if she decides that she doesn't want to be my mommy? What do we do then? What if she leaves? What if she moves to another house just with Simone?"

Jesus. I felt her words like a punch to the gut.

I moved my chair closer to hers and reached out to her cheeks, clearing off the sugar with a napkin. "That won't happen, Bella. I promise."

"How can you promise?"

She was right. How could I? This wasn't my life. I had no business going around making promises. I also didn't know how to explain to her that some adults were dependable, unlike her own mother. I'd seen Scarlett with Bella. She cared about the little girl as much as we did. She was attached to her.

"You're right. It's not my place to promise that. It's something only your dad and Scarlett can do. But from what I've observed, I don't think Scarlett will move anywhere else. She won't leave you."

"Okay, I believe you," Bella said easily. And just like that, she went back to her beignet, her cheeks quickly covered in powdered sugar once more.

I took another bite of my own beignet, and then Bella shocked the hell out of me by asking, "Uncle Xander, did you ever think about asking a lady friend to live with you?"

I looked up at her and stammered, "N-No."

"Why not? It's awesome. Daddy's so much happier since Scarlett is with us. He smiles a lot more. You could use some smiling. You really don't smile a lot."

If she was going to call me a Grinch, too, or a grump, like some sexy candymaker I knew...

Bella pushed her plate away, looking at me with that serious expression again. She truly reminded me of Isabeau a bit. "Uncle Xander, you've never lived with a lady friend?"

"No." I was amazed that I was having this conversation with my niece.

"Then how can you know you don't like it?"

"Kiddo, sometimes you don't have to try out a thing to know you wouldn't like it."

"But that makes no sense! I always used to say, 'I don't like broccoli,' but I tasted it once, and it was awesome! But it was green and butt-ugly, and I always thought, 'I won't like it.'"

"It's not really the same thing."

"How so?"

I had to choose my words carefully. I didn't want to shut down the conversation and tell her it was none of her business or that it was adult stuff. It wasn't my style. I always took her questions seriously and tried to break them down into responses she could understand. But this time, it was more difficult than usual.

"Sometimes you have an inkling of the things you like. After you've spent a lot of time living by yourself like me, you get used to life being that way."

"Just because you get used to something doesn't mean something else can't be good," Bella said, and for a second, I almost forgot that she wasn't a teenager but still a kid. *Where did she get this wisdom?*

"That's true. But when some things involve a big change, you have to consider it very carefully before making said change."

"But you've considered it forever. You're old."

I winked at her. "And proud of it. The older I get, the more I know what I like."

"You always say that you don't like the Christmas season because everyone goes gaga. But you were happy at the open house with the eggnog and with Bailey. She's so awesome, don't you think? And her pralines are the best. The. Best! Scarlett says we can make some, but they won't be as good as hers. But we're going to try anyway."

I sure as shit couldn't give myself away in front of my niece. I couldn't lie to her, but she didn't need to know everything that was going on in my life. She wouldn't be able to wrap her mind around it. Hell, *I* could barely do that. So I did the next best thing, and changed the topic. I asked her about her favorite Harry Potter book, and she lit up, immediately talking about book 3.

After finishing the beignets, I took her home. I spotted Chad's car in front of the house, which meant he and Scarlett were back from their date already. If not, I would've spent the time with Bella until they returned.

"Great timing," my brother said as we stepped inside. He was carrying Simone on his shoulder. Apparently, she was such a great sleeper that they even took her on their dates.

Scarlett was right next to him, smiling at Bella. "You still have some powdered sugar here and here." She pointed to the corners of her mouth.

"I'm going to clean up upstairs," Bella replied.

"Sure. And then it's time for you to go to bed," Chad said.

I always wondered how that was even possible after a rush of sugar, but it was none of my business. As I'd told Bella, I was single and planned to stay that way.

But for the first time in my life, it sounded hollow to me.

After Bella went upstairs, Chad put his arm around Scarlett's waist. "Was she okay?"

"Of course. My niece is always okay," I said with a wink. I debated telling him about our conversation, but even though she hadn't specifically told me, I knew it was in confidence. She wouldn't want me to blab about it. "We had a good catch-up."

"What exactly did you have to catch up about?" Chad asked.

"Yeah, you two just caught up with things at the open house," Scarlett added.

"Bella and I never run out of things to talk about," I said in a conclusive tone. "And I am not spilling the beans. Everything I talk about with Bella stays between the two of us."

"See, that's why she likes him so much. He never blabs."

I frowned. "Who does?"

Chad started to laugh. "That, brother, is something I won't tell you. I do need my sources, after all."

Right. Having a kid was clearly complicated. You wanted to give them the leeway but also wanted to know if they needed help or were in trouble. But

Bella wasn't in trouble, so I felt completely at ease with my decision not to share anything with them. "Have a good evening, you two."

After I left their house and climbed into my car, I glanced at my phone.

I'd fought the impulse to text Bailey the whole evening. But now, I was alone and wanted to know how she was doing. Was she thinking about me as often as I was about her?

Xander: Home yet? My beignet date was a success. I just dropped Bella off at home, happy and smiling.

She didn't reply, so I simply drove off. But on the way home, my phone lit up and I checked it.

Bailey: No, I'm still at the confectionery. We had a strong wind, and a branch fell from the tree right on top of the storage room.! It's all a mess.

I instantly called her.

"Are you okay?" I asked as soon as she picked up. I couldn't stand anything happening to her. My thoughts spiraled out of control just thinking about it. But she'd texted me and answered her phone. I took both those things as a good sign.

"Yes."

"You weren't hurt?"

"No, neither me nor anyone from the crew, thank goodness. We all heard a loud crack, so we got out of the building just in time."

"Did you call the firemen?"

"Yes, they were here an hour ago. They've removed the branch. We're just trying to see what we can salvage from all the boxes that were inside." Her voice was trembling. "There's also a lot of debris, so we need to clean that up first."

"Why didn't you tell me?" I asked her, starting to feel irrationally angry.

"Why would I?" she replied defensively.

It was a good question.

"I could've hired a team to help you."

"There was no time, Xander. And anyway, my team is here. Listen, I have to go."

"Sure."

She hung up the next second.

Instead of driving home, I turned, heading in the direction of the confectionery. She had mentioned that her team was there, but clearly they were in over their heads. Without hesitating, I called Beckett.

"Hey, brother," I greeted him.

"I gather your date with our favorite niece is over?"

"Yep."

"Want to hang out, go to one of Julian's bars?"

"No, listen. And before you interrupt me, let me finish what I have to say. There was an incident at the confectionery. A tree fell or something. Anyway, they need help cleaning up and seeing what part of the inventory can still be used. I'm going there to help. I haven't been able to assess the situation myself yet, but I think they need all hands on deck. Do you have time to spare?"

"Man, that was a long-ass way to just say, 'Can you come and lend us your muscle?'"

"Whatever. Can you?"

"Sure, why not? I don't have anything else to do. All for dear Bailey, huh?"

I growled. "Beckett, don't start."

"Oh, come on, man. You mauled that poor woman in our parents' kitchen. I thought some alien had snatched your body and replaced it, because that is definitely not like you."

"I know," I replied.

"Oh, okay, you do know. I figured you didn't even realize you were acting out of character—which, by the way, is a good thing, okay? So, keep doing it."

"Duly noted. Maybe Anthony has time too."

"You think there's that much damage?"

"Again, the more of us there are, the faster we'll finish."

"Sure. We should call Zachary there too. He's always good at these types of things."

"Good idea. Can you check if both have time?"

"But see, that would put me in a conundrum because then they'd ask, 'Why the hell are you even doing this?' And without your permission," he said very sardonically, "I can't tell them about the eggnog incident."

"Beckett, you're getting on my last nerve," I gritted out.

"Yeah, I had the feeling that I was on thin ice already. Sure, count on me. I'll ask them if they have time and tell them to direct any questions to you. How about that?"

"That's perfect," I replied, knowing full well that both Zachary and Anthony would instantly put two and two together. But at this point, I didn't really care. What did it matter if they did? Why should I hide? Hell, maybe they could even chip in with advice—although Julian and Chad were probably the best at this dating thing.

Chapter Thirteen

Xander

The second I reached the confectionery, I realized that I could've gotten the whole family here to help and we would still be here for hours. It wasn't just a branch that fell off—the whole tree sort of disintegrated. I knew for a fact that the place had an inspection a few months ago, inside and out, so this was a little alarming. There were huge tire tracks, probably from the firefighters. A window was smashed in too. At least the roof was untouched.

Normally, all I'd think about was the financial impact in a situation like this. But oddly enough, my only concern was for Bailey and how I could help her. Thank God she was physically okay.

I walked inside to a cacophony of sounds. Everyone was inside the storage room, cleaning: Bailey, Avery, and two guys.

"Hello," I called to announce my presence.

Bailey immediately straightened up. "Xander!"

Avery spun around too. They both looked exhausted.

"I'm here to help out," I told them. "Beckett will be here soon. Possibly Anthony and Zachary too."

I turned to the two guys, who looked really young. They seemed to be in their early twenties. "I'm Xander LeBlanc."

"Hi, sir. Such an honor to meet you," one of them said. "I'd shake your hand, but I'm covered in dust and debris."

"Don't worry about it. What do you need me to do?" I asked.

"We have a lot of shelves here, and the branch fell right through the window, completely smashing them," Bailey explained.

"We're trying to gauge which shelves we can reuse," the second guy said.

"And if any of the big boxes have intact praline boxes inside," Avery added. Now that she mentioned them, I noticed five huge carton boxes under the window. "But first we need to clean this out properly."

"Do you know how to clean?" Bailey asked. It was such an honest question that I couldn't help but burst out laughing.

"As a matter of fact, I do."

"Then I'm going to bring another broom for you."

"I'll come with you and get it."

Avery turned to the guys. "Let's continue where we left off."

Bailey stepped in front of me, walking toward the back.

"Bailey," I said, grabbing her arm and slightly turning her around. "Are you okay? You seem on edge."

She slumped her shoulders. "It's just been a long day. But we'll be done soon." She was starting to shake lightly. "I'm just a bit tired. If we don't finish today..."

"Bailey." I cupped her face with both hands, tilting her head up. "We will finish—"

"Because I have a lot of deliveries tomorrow."

"I can have someone else do the deliveries," I assured her.

"But that's the thing. I actually like doing the deliveries. People expect me to be in some places."

She was working herself into a frenzy again, so I tilted her head up even more and leaned closer. "If you don't stop, I'll kiss you."

She blinked and started to laugh. "Why would you do that?"

"To take your mind off it."

She smiled. "Oh, you're good. It really would. I mean, look at this. Simply mentioning it made me forget about everything for a split second."

"Listen to me. We'll figure out the details, okay? If we don't manage to finish the cleanup tonight, you and Avery don't have to coordinate everything on your own."

"But we've always done that. I know it's part of the Orleans Conglomerate, but it just never mattered before."

"This is an emergency, so things are different."

"We've had emergencies in the past." Her tone was playful, as were her eyes.

"But I didn't know about it." Then I growled, leaning closer. "I didn't know you."

"Hm. So, you'd be doing this as a special favor?" she murmured, looking at my lips.

"I just don't want to see you out of sorts," I admitted.

She swallowed hard. I nearly kissed her, but then my brothers' unmistakable voices filtered in.

"Hi," Beckett said. "I'm Beckett. This is Anthony and Zachary. We're Xander's brothers."

I took in a deep breath and stepped back. *What is wrong with me?*

"We're going to need more brooms," I said.

"Let's go to the supply room."

She seemed more at ease as we got the brooms and other cleaning supplies. Her shoulders were no longer up to her ears, and her frown wasn't as deep. I'd made progress. And yet all I wanted was to take her home and make sure she was okay.

But first things first: we had to clean up.

"Fancy seeing you already here, brother," Zachary said. He looked between me and Bailey, and I knew he'd already figured it out. My brother was intuitive that way. "Avery already instructed us on cleaning this place as well as possible."

"We'll do our very best," Beckett added.

"It's not my strong suit," Anthony confessed. "But as my brother pointed out, we LeBlancs always give our best."

Zachary looked at the two of them. "When you clean, steer clear of any shards or sharp edges."

I was glad he was here. Zachary was really good in emergencies.

Once everyone had a designated task, we jumped into the fray. Thankfully, with all of us helping, we finished much quicker than I'd thought.

"Zachary, you've got mad organizational skills," Avery said a few hours later, once the room looked decent again.

"Thanks. The joke in the family is that when there's an emergency, everyone wants me in charge."

"That's something we always say to each other. I didn't know you actually knew," I told him.

"Unlike you, brother," Beckett cut in, "the rest of us don't keep secrets from one another. We say exactly what we think."

Beckett and Anthony always marched to the beat of their own drum.

"Your kitchen and ovens are untouched, right?" Beckett asked, slipping into business mode as he addressed Bailey and Avery.

"I believe so," Bailey replied.

"Well, if not, we can always try and accommodate everything in our bakeries," Beckett went on. "My team can contact you tomorrow."

That gave me an idea. Beckett was running the bakeries section of the Orleans Conglomerate. They could take over the praline business too. I would have to actually run some numbers before I brought the idea to my brother, though. But it had merits.

"Thanks for the offer, but I don't think it's necessary," Bailey told him.

"It's best if we just call it a night, don't you think?" Avery said.

"I think that's a good idea," Bailey agreed. "Guys, how can we thank you?"

"I want pralines," Anthony said. Zachary and Beckett nodded too.

Bailey grabbed boxes from the untouched shelves, handing one to each of them.

Anthony immediately ate two. "I always forget how good these are." Then he pointed at me and said, "Don't you dare shut this down. I don't want LeBlanc & Broussard pralines to stop existing."

The mood instantly changed. Anthony usually had the best sense of humor, but clearly he was exhausted. He looked once around the room and cleared his throat. "I saw this joke going differently. I take it back."

"Yeah, that's not going to work," Beckett replied. Uncharacteristically for him, he sounded a bit pissed.

"We're all tired," Zachary concluded. "I think it's best that we leave before someone makes things even more awkward." He looked pointedly at Anthony. Whenever Zachary was present, he read the room and took care of things. Most of the time, I didn't even have to pull out the big brother card.

"All right, everyone, let's move," I said.

As we all prepared to leave the building, Avery told Bailey, "I'll drop you off." Glancing at me, she added, "We came with one car today."

"I'll take Bailey home," I said without further ado.

Both sisters looked at me in unison.

"You will?" Bailey asked in wonder. Thankfully, my brothers were far enough away that they couldn't hear the conversation.

Avery just laughed and said, "Hey, it's your call. But your house really is out of my way." Clearly she was fighting laughter.

Even though I had no idea where Avery lived, even I knew that was a poor excuse.

"Riiight." Now Bailey was openly laughing. "And I'm sure it's totally on Xander's way."

"I'll take care of Bailey." I put an arm around her shoulders.

Avery seemed to relax, and she smiled at us. "Have a good evening. And thanks a lot for coming here with your brothers."

Once everyone left, Bailey locked up, and I led her to my car.

After we got in, I asked, "Are you hungry?"

"You didn't see me stuffing my face with pralines when we were working?"

"No. When did you even do that?"

She winked. "I can be sneaky if I want."

"But you didn't have to be."

She shrugged. "Are you hungry?"

"No, I'm good."

"How was your evening with Bella?"

"You really want to talk about that?"

"Yes, please. Just take my mind off everything."

I grinned at her. "I still have a better idea about how to do that."

"Yeah, but you can't kiss and drive, okay? So start with a story about your beignet date."

On the drive to her house, I told her about my conversation with Bella—leaving out the part where she asked me if I wanted to move in with someone. But I did tell her about Bella's question about Scarlett.

"Oh, that sweet girl," Bailey said as we neared her house. "It must be hard to have such a strange relationship with your own mom. I can't imagine."

"You're close to yours?" I asked.

"Yes, very. She and Dad were always there for us. They worked a lot, but we didn't feel abandoned in any way, or like they didn't care about us."

She'd picked that up about Sarah from the little I'd told her. It still bugged me how nonchalant she was about her own daughter. At least it was good to know I wasn't being overly judgmental when it came to her.

"I can't believe we're here already," Bailey said.

"Yep. Your Uber driver got you here as fast as possible." When I turned off the engine, I got out of the car at the same time as she did and walked with her to her front door.

"Want to come in?" she asked.

I swallowed hard.

Every fiber of my being wanted to go inside with her. I'd been obsessing about it for the past few hours, but I knew it wasn't a good idea.

"Not smart."

"Oh, right." She laughed nervously, turning around. "My bad, sorry. I'll just go in."

"Bailey."

She stopped in the act of jutting the key into her door. I put a hand on her waist—I fucking needed the contact—and brought my mouth to her ear. "It's not because I don't want to."

"Isn't it?" she whispered.

"No. All I want to do is..." I pressed my fingers into her waist, leaning my forehead against the side of her head. "It's you. Being alone with you."

I exhaled sharply, taking a step back. She turned to face me, licking her lips.

With a growl, I kissed her. Fucking hell, how I needed her lips. She sighed in surprise but opened up instantly. Then I couldn't hold back. I needed to explore her so fucking much. I wanted to make her moan right here on her front porch. I deepened the kiss, moving her until her back was flat against the entrance door. I felt both her hands on my chest, then moving upward until they finally rested on my shoulders. She hummed, and I drank up every sound, every reaction. I pulled her even closer, resting my hands on her hips. She whimpered when I pressed her against the zipper of my pants. I was semihard, and she could feel it.

Groaning, I took a step back. "You taste delicious."

Bailey covered her mouth with her hand, giggling. "This was unexpected." On a sigh, she added, "Xander, look, I know what I said yesterday, but I'm... God, I'm so confused."

Confused. I didn't like the sound of that. I didn't want to take advantage of her.

"And now with the Christmas season going on," she continued, "I have so much to do."

That gave me an idea. Thanksgiving was coming soon, and after that, the Réveillon dinners started.

"I have a proposition for you."

She interlaced her hands, looking at me apprehensively. "Yes?"

"Let's go to a Réveillon dinner."

"Ohhh, I haven't been to one in years. Our parents took us when I was in high school."

"Then that's settled. I'll make arrangements."

"But why?"

"So we can discuss everything that's confusing you."

Of course I couldn't keep my distance, so I took two steps toward her.

"You think that needs an entire dinner?" she asked.

"Yes. We can debate every point very thoroughly," I pointed out.

Her eyes widened a bit. "Okay. I'll make a list of everything that confuses me."

I frowned. "There are so many things, you need a list?"

She looked down at her feet and then back up. "I'm not sure."

"Then think of everything because I want you to be *damn* sure."

She shuddered. "Will it be at LeBlanc & Broussard?"

"No. I like to support the family business when I can, but there are too many eyes and ears there."

She threw her head back, laughing, and then straightened up. "With all your brothers owning half the Quarter, I don't think any place is safe."

"I'll find something," I assured her.

"Okay, then, I'll wait for your text."

"Sure. Enjoy Thanksgiving."

"And you," she replied.

Chapter Fourteen
Bailey

Thanksgiving usually went by in a whirl, and it was no different this year. But as we headed out to Mom and Dad's house in Baton Rouge, all thought of work simply went away, and we had a very relaxing evening. Because Mom was originally from New Jersey, she cooked meals that weren't Southern in the slightest. She always said that we all stuffed our faces with Southern food all day long anyway, and she was right.

"You girls seem more tense than usual," Mom commented after we'd cleared the table.

"We just have a lot going on," Avery said, "with that tree and everything."

"But you said the LeBlancs are already on top of it, right?" Mom asked.

"Yes, they are," I replied.

"So that means they want to keep it going, right?" Dad asked in a rather brusque tone.

"They need it in good shape if they sell it off," Avery said, then glanced at me questioningly.

I wasn't sure what to tell her. Xander and I were circling each other. Toeing a fine line. There were many ways to say it. And I was certain that had a lot to do with why the LeBlancs were getting involved in this instead of simply having us deal with it as usual.

"It's all going to be fine," Avery said. "I'm sure of it."

"Oh, hon, you're always the eternal optimist," Mom said.

"Yes, and I don't get that from you, Mom, do I? You could learn a thing or two from me, you know."

She laughed, then kissed Avery's temple. "No, you're right, I should. I've lived my whole life thinking that something bad was going to happen, and look at me. I'm nearing retirement, and life is as good as ever."

We all burst out laughing. Mom and Dad glanced at each other. Growing up, I'd always looked at them and thought, *"That's the kind of love I want to have. If I don't have that, I'd rather not have anything."* And yet all these years had passed by, and I hadn't found anything even remotely similar. Some days I asked myself if it was even still possible.

Damn, that's no way to think. I needed to borrow some of my sister's optimism.

As was tradition for every Thanksgiving, we stayed up until very late, and it was well past midnight when I arrived home. I took a quick shower and immediately went to bed. Then I remembered I had to set the alarm clock.

That was when I realized that Xander had texted me.

Xander: Are you still awake?

My heart started to beat more rapidly. He'd sent it just a few minutes ago. Maybe he was still available to talk or message.

Bailey: Yes.

I expected him to reply, but he called me instead.

"Good evening."

I *loved* that sexy voice.

"Hey."

"How was your Thanksgiving?"

"It was really nice. I loved catching up with my parents. Yours?"

"Delicious and loud."

I laughed. "Why do I feel like that describes everybody in the LeBlanc-Broussard mansion?"

"Because it does. There was only one thing missing."

"What?"

"You."

Oh, goodness. What exactly did he mean? That he would've liked me to join his family for Thanksgiving? Nah, that couldn't be.

"And by the way, I've made reservations for our Réveillon dinner," he added.

"Where?"

"A restaurant that you'll love in the French Quarter. Can't give you any details, though."

"Why not? I want to look it up online."

"Doesn't have a web page. In fact, most people don't even know it exists."

"Huh. Now I'm starting to worry that you're going to lure me into a dark alley and have your way with me."

He growled. "Don't say that twice or I might come knocking at your door right now."

Heat coursed through me, and I realized that I actually wanted that. God, I'd never been so reckless.

"When are we going?" I asked, trying to redirect my thoughts.

"Next Friday."

I grinned into the darkness. "That's great. It gives me enough time to put together a perfect outfit."

"Bailey, you'll look gorgeous no matter what."

I shimmied under the sheets, yawning.

"I'll let you sleep."

"But I love talking to you."

I yawned again, though, and he laughed.

"Good night, Bailey."

"Good night."

But after hanging up, I didn't go to sleep. I was too excited about our up-coming date, so I went to my favorite online shop. It had super-fast delivery.

I eyed a dark green dress that was to die for. It was a bit expensive, but I could definitely afford it. I wanted to spoil myself. And since I was already splurging on a dress, I also added shoes. One could never have enough shoes.

I was going to knock him off his feet. I was sure of it.

Chapter Fifteen

Bailey

My dark green dress molded to my curves a little bit too much, showing off a lot of cleavage, but I loved it. I'd paired it with black high heels and was searching in my closet for a coat.

"Can you come back in front of the camera?" Avery asked.

We'd been on a video call the entire time I got ready. She kept giving me tips and tricks on how to style myself.

"Yep," I said, moving over in front of the phone.

"You're a knockout. And I'm not saying that just because I'm biased, which of course I am. You're super, super beautiful."

"Thanks, sis."

Avery tilted her head. "What do you think will happen tonight?"

I fiddled with my thumbs, shrugging. "We're going to enjoy a fantastic dinner. And talk."

"Looking like that, he's going to maul you before you even finish dinner."

"Avery!" But I was sort of hoping she was right.

Wasn't that crazy? How could I be so attracted to a man who planned to turn our lives upside down? And held so many beliefs that were different from mine?

Well, perhaps that wasn't strictly true. We differed in many ways, but we had one thing in common: we each cared deeply about our family.

"All right, I've got to go. He's going to be here any second now."

As if on cue, the doorbell rang.

"Okay, bye. Have fun." She sent me an air kiss before disconnecting the call.

I was downright jittery as I put the phone in my small clutch bag, then threw on my coat before opening the door. Xander stood there wearing only a suit, no coat or anything. I would forever be grateful that this man's inner temperature seemed to be much higher than normal because I loved seeing him in a suit.

"Good evening, Bailey."

"Hi!" I almost squeaked. *Oh goodness. This is an interesting start.*

"Ready to go?"

"Yep. I've got everything I need."

He looked me up and down, his eyes settling on my feet. "Are you sure you won't be cold?"

"That's debatable, but I'm assuming we'll be indoors most of the time."

"Obviously. I'll find a parking spot nearby, and if there isn't one, then I'll drop you off as near as possible to the restaurant."

I stilled. All of that for my convenience? That was something, wasn't it?

"That sounds like a great plan."

He motioned for me to walk to his car. I felt even more nervous than before, remembering the last time he'd seen me. This door had seen some seriously sexy action.

"I keep thinking about your parents and grandparents in the same house. I never realized that there are still families who live together the way yours does," I said once we were in the car.

"I find it unusual too. My grandparents weren't fans in the beginning."

"So, how did your parents win them over? I can't imagine anyone convincing Isabeau to do something she doesn't want to."

He chuckled. "No, but she started to slow down in the past few years, and she realized that. Whatever we might say about Isabeau, she isn't one to lie to herself. She spent a lot of time with Celine anyway, so they figured that living together wouldn't be a huge change. That house is big enough that everyone has their private space."

"It's one of my favorites in the Garden District."

"How so?"

"Because it's gorgeous but somehow not ostentatious. Despite its size, it's actually cozy."

He nodded. "Cozy. Never thought of it like that, but it's a good description. Are your parents doing okay?"

"Yes, they are. Mom managed to take time off for Thanksgiving. We're super grateful for that, though she said she'll probably have to take a nursing shift on Christmas Day in exchange. It was nice catching up with her and Dad. Now, tell me more about the restaurant. If it's as good as you say it is, how can they keep it a secret?"

Xander kept looking at the road, but I saw his face transform into a smile.

"It's one of the best-kept secrets in the French Quarter. It's on the second floor of a building. There's no sign or anything. The owner goes by the name of D, and that's it."

"What? Come on, you must know his name."

"I don't. I didn't try very hard to find out either. If the man wants to keep his identity a secret, who am I to ruin his fun? He's been running that place for forty years with a small crew. He's got three Michelin stars but doesn't advertise it at all."

"That is insane," I said.

"I know."

"So, you've been there before?"

"Yes, once. The food is delicious. They only have five tables, though."

"And you got one?" I asked incredulously.

"Yeah."

"Okay, I need more details. How did that happen?"

"I did D a favor once, and he remembers."

"Do you always like being this mysterious?"

He winked. "Yes."

I was seeing Xander in an entirely new light. This man was always focused on whatever brought the best results and being efficient, yet he'd done someone a favor and didn't even brag about it. I was starting to like him more and more.

We arrived very quickly on Decatur Street, and Xander even found a parking lot.

"We need to walk a couple minutes from here. Are you good to do that?"

I nodded. "I'm not made out of sugar."

"I just don't want you to be cold or uncomfortable."

"I'm good. Besides, I want to stretch my legs a bit."

"All right." He pulled into the lot.

I got out as soon as he'd parked and took in a deep breath. The air was warmer than I'd expected. Smiling, I looked around. I didn't come to the Quarter that often.

"I like your smile," Xander said.

I startled at his voice. I hadn't realized he'd already come over to my side.

"I like this evening. It's got a good vibe."

Jazz music filtered throughout the streets. Sometimes it seemed nearer and sometimes farther away. Maybe it was just a trick of the wind.

Decatur Street was one of my favorites in New Orleans; it wasn't as touristy, and things moved more at my pace. Even though Xander had warned me, I was still surprised that there was no sign of a restaurant whatsoever when we reached the building. It was bright red with white shutters and had a very small balcony with a white railing.

"Where's the entrance?" I asked.

"Right through here." He pointed to the small nondescript door next to the main entrance and opened it, revealing a very narrow staircase.

"The plot thickens. This is so exciting."

Xander laughed. "I thought you might appreciate this place. It was what sold D on giving us a table at the last minute."

I looked over my shoulder as I went up, and what do you know? I caught Xander LeBlanc staring at my ass. Well, at my coat, really. Although he could probably see the contour of my ass if he really looked because the coat was snug. It was still buttoned up.

"I thought you convinced him using your prowess."

"My prowess?" he parroted, looking up at me.

"That's right," I countered.

"My *abilities* helped. But they had to bring in an extra table for us, something he never does."

At the end of the staircase, there was another small door, and I immediately opened it.

"This is so cozy," I murmured as we both went inside.

There were only a few tables for two throughout the smaller room, with a small fireplace to the right of the window. The fire was crackling, and they'd put candles on the mantelpiece. Soft piano music played in the background.

Xander was looking at me with a curious expression when I faced him after taking it all in.

"I love it!" I gushed.

He smiled instantly. "I'm happy to hear that. I'll take your coat."

Xander watched me intently as I unbuttoned my coat and then slipped it off.

As I handed it to him, I heard him inhale sharply and immediately glanced up at him. He was checking out my cleavage now.

So, this was the evening where he finally forgot his manners, huh? Although, if I thought about it, he'd already shown me that side of him when we were making eggnog... and when he'd kissed me against my door. Still, this was a bit different because we were in public. I liked that he couldn't hold himself in check.

After he took my coat, I turned away. There was no way for me to hide my smug smile anymore.

There was a door opposite the fireplace, and it immediately opened. A man who looked to be in his late seventies stepped in.

"Xander, this must be your lovely lady."

"Hi, D," Xander said.

"Your lovely lady," huh? I was liking this more and more.

"That's for you." He pointed to a table close to the fire. "If it gets too hot, let me know and I'll—"

"I'll move it if necessary," Xander assured him. "Thank you for everything, D."

"Sure. Why don't you two sit down, and I'll start serving right away."

"Thank you. Your restaurant is very cozy. I can't believe I didn't know about it," I said.

D smiled at me, and it transformed his whole face. "My wife and I started it many years ago. It was just a place where we served food to our friends. Then we asked our friends to send friends, and it slowly became a restaurant. But we wanted to keep it small, so we only took reservations based on recommendations. I lost her ten years ago, and I'm doing everything on my own, so I don't want more people anyway. No need."

My heart ached when his eyes turned sad at the mention of his wife's passing.

"I'll bring drinks to you," he said, and then he went back through the door.

"He does everything?" I double-checked with Xander.

"Yep."

"But this is a lot of work for him."

"He assured me that he can do it, but there's a catch: it means you only get what he's bringing you. You noticed he didn't take our order?"

"That's right."

D returned with a bottle of wine. "This is the house wine. My brother-in-law makes it all the way out in Charleston."

I barely bit back a laugh. *All the way out,* huh? "I'm surprised you're serving wine. I thought maybe you'd pull out some Pimm's or Sazeracs."

He shook his head, looking as if I'd mortally offended him. "That doesn't go with my food."

Mental note: don't crack any more jokes.

After he poured our wine, he went to the other tables, refilling their glasses before disappearing into the kitchen.

I looked at the fireplace for a few seconds and sighed.

"I so wish my fireplace worked," I confessed. "I love them."

"I have one in my penthouse," Xander replied.

My heart stuttered, and my pulse went up a few notches. "Already trying to lure me back to your place, huh?"

"Doing my very best."

Holy shit. Okay, this wasn't just a flirty Réveillon dinner. It was full-on seductive mode.

"Wait... did you say penthouse?"

"Yes, in the business district."

"Is it an electric fireplace?"

"No. It burns wood, but it's modern."

"Doesn't matter. Fire is fire." I took a sip of the wine and then another one. "I'm already sold on this place."

"Wait until you taste the food."

"You certainly know how to wine and dine someone," I said carefully. I was fishing for information. Was this his usual MO? Did he impress everyone the way he was impressing me? I had to be stealthy, though, because I'd be super embarrassed if he caught on.

"I don't usually do this," he said instantly.

I busied myself by looking at my glass. "You don't?" I was holding my breath.

"No, Bailey. I really don't."

I looked up at him. His eyes were fixed on me.

"I usually don't even—"

But he never managed to finish that sentence because D came up to us with corn soup. He simply put it down in front of us and left without an explanation.

"I haven't eaten this in a while," I said, then dug in.

It only took a spoonful to understand why D had three Michelin stars. It was creamy and a bit garlicky, but not too strong. There was also some smokiness that fit perfectly.

My shoulders dropped of their own accord, and a calmness came over me as we sat and ate comfortably. I leaned my head back, smiling for no reason before taking another spoonful, just enjoying the evening.

"I like seeing you this relaxed," Xander said.

He touched my leg under the table, and I stilled, hoping my body wasn't going to react in an inappropriate way. No such luck. My panties instantly felt superhot, but at least the bright side was that Xander couldn't tell.

"That's my plan for this evening," he continued.

"To r-relax me?" I stuttered.

He had a mischievous glint in his eyes. I thought he might have an idea of what was going on between my thighs.

"Yes."

"You're on your merry way to doing just that," I assured him.

The evening was amazing. The second appetizer was shrimp, and it tasted even better than the soup. D served it on a bed of spiraled carrots and zucchini, which weren't my favorite vegetables, but these were so delicious that I could eat a truckload. The main course was turkey breast with ham and pureed potatoes.

"It's a good thing D doesn't allow people to order."

"Why?" Xander asked.

"Because I would never have ordered any of this, and it's amazing."

"I agree."

"Want more wine?"

"Want me to get drunk?" he teased.

"No, I just want you to open up so I can get some info out of you."

"Such as?"

"How you discovered D and what you usually do with your dates."

Chapter Sixteen
Bailey

Oh crap. Xander might have only sipped from his wine this whole evening, but D had refilled my glass a few times. I wasn't drunk by any means—I didn't even feel really tipsy—but clearly I'd had enough to speak out of turn. I pressed my lips together. "That didn't come out right."

"Bailey," he said, reaching over the table for my hand. Heat instantly coursed through my entire body when he laced our fingers together. The gesture felt so intimate. "Listen, I'd rather not talk about that."

"I'm not even sure why I wanted to know," I admitted.

"That doesn't matter. All that matters is that it would put you at ease. I don't have any secrets. I'd just prefer that we enjoy this evening. As to the other thing, that's a secret I'll never share. It's not mine."

We didn't get to talk much more because D returned with dessert. He'd made Christmas trifle and doused it in booze for all it was worth. It tasted more like amaretto than cake, but it was amazing.

"This has been spectacular. It's like every course goes with the next one," I murmured as I finished my dessert.

Xander was looking at me intently. "You didn't say anything about that list. The things that confuse you."

"Oh... I don't remember any of it." Blushing, I added, "I didn't even make the list."

"I want you to be comfortable with me."

"The dinner totally did the trick." I flashed a seductive/tipsy smile.

"I want you, Bailey."

Ohhhh, that totally worked for me, judging by how my body felt.

"I want you more than anything I've ever wanted in my life." He was keeping his voice low, and good thing he was, because otherwise, all the other couples could hear us.

I was too speechless to say anything else, so I just nodded.

There was a hot glint in his eyes, and he nudged my leg with his under the table. "Do you want us to ask for another dessert or more wine?"

"No, I need a bit of fresh air." I needed to walk off the wine, if that was even possible.

A few minutes later, we were out on Decatur Street. The bright side to drinking so much wine was that I wasn't cold at all.

"Someone's really warm, huh?" Xander asked me.

"Yep."

"No need for me to warm you up, then."

I looked at him out of the corner of my eye. "If you insist, I won't say no."

"I do."

"The jazz music is closer now. Pity they aren't playing Christmas carols."

"What's your favorite carol?" he asked, amusement thick in his voice.

"'White Christmas.' Yours?"

"I don't have a favorite one."

"You just hate all of them equally?"

"I don't hate them," he said with a grin. "I'm just not as into them as everyone else." He straightened up. "Wait a second. I know where this saxophonist is. He's on Toulouse, next to Café Beignet."

"How would you know that?"

"Because I'm there sometimes with Bella, and I recognize his way of playing. Want to head over there?"

"Sure. I love the celebratory feeling between Thanksgiving and Christmas," I said. He gave me his arm, and I hooked mine around it without a second thought, putting my head slightly on his shoulder. I couldn't blame this on the wine; I simply wanted to be with him. "It's officially acceptable to start enjoying all things Christmas."

He kissed the top of my head, and I felt as if someone doused me in warm water. "As if you need it to be official."

"I don't, but everything comes to life with lights."

"It does make the city look friendlier."

I instantly straightened up. "Will you look at that. An aspect of Christmas that you like."

He chuckled. "I think you're starting to rub off on me."

As we walked farther down the street, I saw the saxophonist, instrument in hand, eyes closed as he played. To my surprise, Xander let go of me and headed to him, interrupting him. He whispered something, and the man nodded. Then Xander put a hundred-dollar bill in the collection bin.

Wow, he was generous. I loved that.

"What was that about?" I asked when he returned, but I had my answer the next second when the music changed.

"He's playing 'White Christmas'!"

"Your favorite." To my utter astonishment, he took my hand and asked, "Want to dance?"

I had no words, so I simply nodded. He put an arm around my waist, moving me in a slow, intimate rhythm that matched the music right there on the corner of Decatur and Toulouse for the whole Quarter to see. But I didn't care, and I had a funny feeling that neither did he. Right now, all that seemed to exist was us, the smell of powdered sugar from Café Beignet, and "White Christmas" filling the air.

Xander pressed his cheek to my forehead, and I was close enough to smell his cologne. It was manly and so very addictive. He didn't say a word as he swayed me to the rhythm of the carol, and neither did I. I was simply enjoying this magical time and being here with this amazing man. It was probably the most romantic moment of my life.

The sounds of the Quarter started to filter in after the music ended. Xander very reluctantly dropped the hand he had on my waist as he took a very small step back, then tilted my chin up. I'd never seen him smile like this.

"This was the most amazing thing ever."

"For me too."

He brushed my hair behind my ear. I licked my lips and caught him looking at my mouth. I wanted nothing more than for him to kiss me. Then he pushed my hair behind my other ear as well. A second later, I realized he'd just been prepping the terrain. He leaned in, sealing his mouth over mine.

The kiss went from tentative to passionate within seconds, and I gave in to all his demands without even thinking. I desperately needed this kiss more than anything else. We were shrouded in the essence of the city, the smell of beignets, the sound of jazz, and I was losing myself to this man a bit more with every breath.

I didn't know how much time had passed when he pulled back. I looked at him through hooded eyes.

"You're shivering."

"I hadn't even realized." Even though my inner temperature was close to boiling, I was cold now. "The effects of the wine are starting to wear off."

He instantly straightened up. *Nooo!* I wanted him to come back and kiss me some more.

"I'll take you home."

My stomach dropped in disappointment, but I didn't say a word.

On the drive home, it was on the tip of my tongue to ask him why he'd changed his mind. Why weren't going to his place? But I needed some more wine to do that.

Once we reached my house, though, Xander asked, "What's wrong?" We got out of the car and walked side by side. "You've been silent the whole way."

"Um..." I laughed nervously, glancing away. I wasn't sure what to tell him. "Nothing. I guess the food made me drowsy."

"Bailey." His voice had dropped an octave. "Don't do that."

"What?" I asked, casting my gaze to him.

"You can tell me anything."

I simultaneously wanted to hold my cards close to my chest and also put them all on the table and be vulnerable with him. The two instincts warred, and the second one won. *Here goes nothing.* "I'm just wondering why you changed your mind."

"About what?"

"Wanting me."

Leaning in, he growled, "I didn't. Why would you think I changed my mind?"

"You said you were going to take me back to your place and show me your fireplace, and then you didn't."

We were silent for a few seconds, and then a smile inched across Xander's face. It got bigger and bigger until it was a full-on smug grin. *Very* smug. "I see."

"I don't," I whispered.

"You think it's because I don't want you."

"Why else?"

He touched my face with the backs of his fingers before cupping my jaw. Then he drew his thumb over my lip. "It's because I want you so damn much that I can't think straight. And if I can't think straight—" He took in a short breath. "—it's dangerous. I didn't want you to feel like I have expectations, like you can't turn me down."

"That didn't even cross my mind."

"I can barely think about anything else."

I was starting to feel warm again. "Really?"

"Yes. And tonight was fucking perfect. Don't for a second think I don't want you."

I didn't wait for him to kiss me this time. Instead, I put my arms around his neck, lacing my fingers behind his head, and tilted toward him. The last thing I was aware of before our mouths met was yet another sexy growl. And then I was completely lost to Xander LeBlanc.

Chapter Seventeen
Xander

I moved her across the porch until we reached the door. I'd barely held back at the restaurant and then during the dance. I had no idea where all that had come from; I just knew it would make her happy. She turned around instantly when she felt the door at her back. I groaned, pressing my fingers into the wood, nearly clawing at it like a wild animal.

I felt her rib cage expand with every breath. I put a hand on her waist, tugging at her coat—I simply couldn't *not* touch her. When she finally opened the door, we barreled inside. She barely managed to close it before I was kissing her again, unbuttoning her coat. I wanted it out of the way. I wanted everything out of the way. I'd fantasized about having this woman naked for weeks.

I pushed her coat off her shoulders and down to the floor. Next thing I knew, she took off her shoes, making her much shorter than me, but it didn't matter. She was perfect just the way she was—every part of her.

I only paused enough to look down at her dress. "I've wanted to take this off all damn night."

She looked down and then back up at me. "Likewise. I like this suit a lot, but I want to see you out of it."

I took a deep breath to calm myself down. "Are you sure?"

"So sure. So, so sure."

"I aim to please."

I immediately shrugged off my jacket, tossing it over her discarded coat. Looking straight at her, I took off my cuff links. I could see her getting turned on right in front of my eyes. It was right there in her body language: the way her eyes darkened and her lips parted; the small shake in her hips. This woman wanted me. I put the cuff links on the shelf next to us, then walked closer to her.

"You'll have to do the rest," I told her.

"I can't wait to oblige."

She started with my buttons, making quick work of them. At the same time, I pulled her dress up to her hips and then nearly exploded in my pants. She was wearing lace garters.

"You look fucking beautiful."

"I bought them especially for tonight."

"For me. No one else can see you wear these. Fucking no one."

"Xander..."

I walked her backward until I'd plastered her against the wooden door again and cupped her face. "I mean it, Bailey."

She shook her head. "I wasn't going to. I don't even wear these usually."

"You have matching panties?" I asked her.

She nodded, and I pushed her dress farther up so I could see them.

"Are you wet?"

She licked her lips, swallowing hard. "Yes."

"How wet? And don't lie to me because I'm going to check."

"Very," she whispered.

I immediately slipped my hand into her panties, rubbing two fingers over her opening. She was so slick that I couldn't even believe it.

"Bailey... Fuck, babe, you're so wet."

"I know," she whimpered.

I slipped a finger inside her. How could I not when she was this wet and ready?

"Oh my God." Panting, she tugged at my shirt and then put her forehead on my chest as if she needed to ground herself. This was already too much for her. But I planned to give her so much more—I knew she could take it. Most of all, she needed it.

I moved my finger in and out, brushing her clit with every stroke. Her whimpers turned to moans. Then I gave her a second finger, and her entire body spasmed. Her shoulders rolled backward, and I captured her mouth. I wanted to feel every one of her moans on my tongue while I had my fingers buried inside her. I was going to make her come like this, right against her door.

I was blind with need for her, but I wanted this orgasm for her first. She was so damn ready, melting in my arms. Her body was taut everywhere I touched her. When her inner muscles started to tighten around my fingers, the moans against my mouth became harder, louder, more intense. I kissed and kissed her relentlessly while I moved my fingers. When I felt her tighten completely, I stilled my movements inside her and simply pressed on her clit. She orgasmed fucking beautifully, clinging to me as she came. Her entire body went soft again instantly. I cupped her ass with my other hand so she could keep her balance without a problem. She was starting to sway from all the pleasure I'd just given her, and I'd barely started.

"Xander," she murmured.

"You're fucking beautiful. You are amazing. I can't get enough of you."

"I need more."

That was music to my ears. "I'll give you everything I have tonight, Bailey. Every fucking thing, I promise. Where's your bedroom?"

She pointed to the door of the living room. "Through there."

I tugged her dress farther up until it was right around her waist. Then I decided to take it off completely. "I love your curves."

She blushed, looking down. "I do like pralines a lot."

"You're perfect. I won't have you think anything else, not for a moment."

I pulled her up to me, needing to feel her close. Her breasts pushed against my chest as I carried her to the bedroom. It was big, and the bed was king-size, which was good. I needed to be able to explore her.

After putting her down, she said, "You."

I was about to ask what she meant, but then she tugged desperately at my shirt, as she'd done in the living room. I knew what she meant. Part of me wanted to let her undress me herself, but I was too desperate for that, so I took care of my own pants and boxers right before she got rid of my undershirt.

Once my clothes were gone, I moved to take off her bra and panties. I'd intended to do it slowly, but I didn't have any patience left. After unhooking her bra and tossing it to the side, I lowered myself to my knees, yanking her panties down as I went. I did take my time with her garters, though.

Looking up at her, I murmured, "I love your thighs. And that pussy is fucking perfect."

She blushed, glancing away, but only for a split second before looking at me again. I put one of her feet on my knee and kissed up her inner thigh until I reached her pussy. I didn't lick, just moved my mouth around, teasing her. Then I put her foot down and repeated the motion with the other one.

Her skin was already so sensitive that she trembled under my touch. She arched backward, pushing her chest out.

"Xander," she cried out. She was on edge again, or perhaps still. I was going to take it off, but not just yet.

I rose to my feet and flipped her around, pushing her hair to one side and kissing her exposed shoulder as she pushed herself back into me. My cock was trapped between our bodies, and I clenched my eyes shut against the sensations threatening to take over me.

I palmed her breasts while I kissed her shoulder and the back of her neck. I liked feeling her body vibrate against mine, the aftershocks of her orgasm. Lowering one hand to her pussy, I dragged my finger over her clit as if I were playing an instrument. She gasped and then pushed her ass into my pelvis even harder. I groaned in her ear, the feeling of her against me making it impossible to think. I wanted to act on impulse and pure instinct, but I needed to make her come again. Only then would I sink inside her.

I kept moving my fingers over her clit, rocking my hips back and forth slightly. The friction against my cock was exquisite. But I stilled first.

"Bailey." My voice was hoarse, I cleared my throat before adding, "I'm clean, babe."

"So am I. On birth control, too, so we don't need a condom. We don't need anything." Her voice was even more desperate than mine. It egged me on.

I grabbed my cock at the base, guiding it between her legs and rubbing it along the length of her pussy.

"Xandeeeer," she mewled, her voice shaking. I barely made out that she'd called my name. This was phenomenal.

In the beginning, it was just enough to ease my need for her, but it only served to intensify that need even more. I played with her clit while I moved back and forth, smiling against her neck when I felt her on the cusp of yet another orgasm. It began much slower than the other one, but the signs were unmistakable. Her skin turned clammy, her body taut. Then she started to tremble—only a bit at first, but then it took over her body. I used my free hand to hold her by her stomach. With the other one, I relentlessly massaged her clit.

I found the rhythm that brought her the most pleasure, and I kept on just like that. She arched back, pushing herself into me. Her head rolled to one side as she cried out my name, her entire body undulating. I wanted to kiss her, but it was impossible in this position, so I simply kept moving my hips and circling her clit until she calmed down and seemed to regain control of her body again.

She straightened up and turned around slowly. Her smile was everything that was right in this world. She kissed my jaw and moved her mouth down my neck. I dropped my head back, enjoying her touch.

I liked her mouth on me, exploring me. She moved to one shoulder, then lowered herself, slowly making a crisscross pattern with her mouth on my torso. She wrapped a hand around my cock and squeezed hard. It felt incredible, but after I'd rubbed against her pussy, this wasn't nearly enough.

"Bailey," I grunted. "I want you. Now." I looked down at her. She was grinning and immediately rose, still squeezing my erection.

Then I kissed her. Yes, I wanted to sink inside her, but I also wanted to kiss her; I needed her mouth more than I could explain. I grabbed her by the ass, bringing her to the height I wanted, then stumbled backward when she started to move up and down, rubbing herself against my cock.

Walking until I reached the wall, I turned around, pushing Bailey against it and then sinking inside her. She responded to my kiss with even more intensity. Being inside her was such a rush that I didn't even need to move at first. I just wanted to feel.

"Your pussy's so damn tight," I whispered in her ear, nibbling at her earlobe. "I love it."

In response, she started to move her hips.

Closing my eyes, I placed my mouth in the crook of her neck. I wanted more contact, and I couldn't focus enough on kissing and fucking at the same time. This woman was messing with my senses in the best way possible.

"Bailey, this is so damn good," I grunted between thrusts.

She whimpered and moaned but didn't reply. She was too far gone for that. We were both chasing the high.

I held her with one hand, and she must have realized I wanted to take the other one away, because she immediately put her hands on my shoulders. I reached between us, pinching her clit.

"Xander, ohhhh!"

I straightened up, wanting to see her. It was precious watching her prepare herself for the wave of pleasure. This moment was so intense that I knew it would claim every single part of me. Miraculously, I didn't have any problems with that. In fact, I was looking forward to losing control completely to Bailey. This thing between us was feral.

I wanted to cup her face, but I needed to be able to touch her far more freely. Against the wall, it was going to be impossible, so I moved her away quickly and carried her straight to the bed.

However, I'd miscalculated the angle to the bed and lost my balance. I dropped her first and then almost collapsed on top of her. But I managed to catch myself in time, breaking my fall by putting my hands forward, at the sides of her shoulders.

She smiled softly. "I made you lose your balance, huh?"

"You make me forget my own name, Bailey." Then I put one of her legs on my shoulder, keeping the other one at my side. I liked this angle; she was spread out good for me. Moving down, I pressed my finger on her clit as I slid inside her all at once. She was wet, and we were both so damn ready for the orgasm.

I moved back and forth with precise and quick thrusts. She grabbed the sheets over her head and began to thrash, rolling her head from left to right. That's why I loved having her here on the bed where she could move freely—neither of us had to worry about balance, and she was able to let loose.

"You're fucking gorgeous." I loved the way her breasts moved as she writhed beneath me.

When her mouth began to tremble, especially her lower lip, I knew she was right there. She came a second later, which sent me over the edge instantly. One minute I was watching her, and the next, I didn't even know where I was. The orgasm ricocheted throughout my body. I blinked rapidly, but my eyes watered. I tried to breathe in deeply, but I couldn't. The pleasure took up too much space in my body to allow for anything else, even air.

I groaned, letting out all the pent-up tension within me. Our sounds filled the room. Neither of us was holding back. My body was a live wire. My back spasmed, and I rolled my shoulders backward and then forward, careful not to collapse over Bailey. At least I had enough self-awareness left for that.

I pulled out of her carefully once she stopped thrashing around. She was smiling, eyes closed. We'd both worked up a sweat. Her hair clung to her cheeks, and I moved it away carefully, kissing that spot of skin. Her smile widened even more as I pulled back. Then she turned her head in my direction, opening her eyes.

"Hmmmm, this was something," she whispered without elaborating. She didn't need to, though. I knew exactly what she was referring to. It wasn't just the pleasure, although that was powerful. There was something else here. The same thing that had made me pop up wherever she'd been over the past few weeks. The same thing that made me constantly think about her.

"Was I too rough earlier when we were against the wall?"

"Oh, you were rough," she said with a frown. Then she grinned again. "And I loved it so freaking much."

"Nothing hurts?" I double-checked.

"Maybe ask me tomorrow. I might have worked up some muscle aches, but I don't mind at all. I haven't had a proper workout since the Christmas season started."

"You count this as a workout?" I asked with a laugh.

"No, but I think it might end up being that." She pushed herself up on her elbows, looking me up and down and then laughing.

"What's so funny?"

"I think you might be too big for my bed."

I frowned. "What are you talking about?"

"I bought the biggest one I could find, and now I have a mountain of a man on it."

Was she implying that I was the first man in her bed? Because the primal side of me fucking liked that.

"Oh, *this* mountain of a man will find a place," I replied.

I shifted us on the bed, but it wasn't as big as I first thought.

"All right, you have a point. But I have an idea." I pulled her on top of me. "See? This works perfectly."

"For what?" she asked, wriggling her eyebrows. "Surely not for sleeping."

"For that, too, later on. For now, I have other things in mind."

CHAPTER EIGHTEEN

X ander

"Hey, Xander," Lydia greeted me when I arrived at the office on Monday morning. "You're a bit late."

"Still on time for the first meeting," I replied. I hadn't left Bailey's house until this morning, going home to change before coming to the office.

"Yes, of course, of course. Listen, I've forwarded you some Christmas invitations you got today."

I raised a brow. "I received more than one in the same day?"

She nodded. "You know how people are. They like to invite anyone who's anyone to those sorts of events."

"You can RSVP that I'm not going."

"Don't you even want to look at them?"

"No, not necessary."

The Christmas events were the bane of my existence. I knew for a fact that most companies had the end of the financial year on the thirty-first. Who had time for all these things? Some of them weren't even corporate parties.

I hadn't attended one in years. The first few years in business, my brothers and I had gone to most of them because we'd been eager to let everyone in New Orleans know that we'd taken over the Orleans Conglomerate. It had been necessary for the town to see the transition. But on the fourth year, I pulled back. There were plenty of us LeBlancs, so we didn't all have to attend.

Some of my brothers were more than happy to keep going. Zachary was a perennial favorite at the parties, as were Anthony and Beckett. Julian had attended many of them, too, before he started spending more and more time behind the counter at his bars. He said he got his socializing fix from there and didn't need the parties, though he attended many events during Carnival season.

As I got into my office, I shrugged out of my suit jacket and grinned for no reason at all when I noticed my cuff links. Bailey had put them on this morning, saying they were her favorite part of my outfit. So I'd worn them.

Out of instinct, I snapped a picture of them and sent it to her.

Bailey: You're wearing the same clothes at the office? Doing the walk of shame?

I replied right away, pacing my office instead of sitting down.

Xander: I went home and changed. I just kept the cuff links.

Bailey: Why?

Xander: Good question. Because you like them so much.

Was it crazy that I wanted her to know this tidbit?

Xander: How is your morning going?

Bailey: Absolutely perfect. I'm a bit sleepy, but someone gave me a lot of good vibes yesterday, so I'm not complaining at all.

I threw my head back, laughing. I gave her good vibes. This woman. In some ways, she felt so completely different from me. Yet in other ways, I felt as if we were exactly the same.

I finally sat at the desk, opening my inbox. Lydia always sent me an email early Monday morning with all the to-dos for the week.

She'd sent me two separate ones this morning. One was simply to-dos, and the other one was the invitations she'd mentioned. The events were listed chronologically along with the addresses so I wouldn't have to sift through every single one to get the details.

I glanced at the list and was preparing to delete the email when one in particular caught my attention: the LUNA Ball. I'd only been there once. It was a fundraiser for art or something mixed in with a fashion show. I hadn't enjoyed it enough to ever return, but I knew someone who'd actually like it—Bailey.

I opened the spreadsheet she'd sent me a while back, and the LUNA Ball wasn't on the list. I started to formulate a plan.

The event was in the evening, which was good—I could get in a full day of work before picking her up and then heading to the event. She also didn't have anything else planned on that evening, at least not according to the spreadsheet.

She would definitely enjoy this, and I'd love nothing more than to watch her. Last time, I'd been there on business. This time, I could just spend the evening with Bailey. The prospect appealed to me more and more the longer I thought about it.

I didn't want to check with Bailey yet, intending to surprise her.

But I did reply to my assistant: **RSVP for two for the LUNA Ball.**

She'd be shocked, but it didn't matter. If Bailey had some other plans, I could always pull out of it.

I did eventually get back to work and managed four hours uninterrupted before I got a phone call from Lydia.

"Hey," she said. "There's this guy named Trudeau who wants to talk to you."

"The name doesn't ring a bell."

"He said it's about the potential sale of the confectionery."

"Oh yeah. Put him through."

This was a pleasant surprise. I'd put out feelers eons ago, but no one had contacted me. I was pleased that someone was interested.

"Hello, my name is Ron Trudeau. You can call me Ron."

"Hi, Ron. I'm Xander LeBlanc."

"I figured it's easier if I just call you."

"Sure. I prefer that to endless emailing too."

"Rumor has it that the Orleans Conglomerate wants to sell the confectionery. It's a small operation, which is exactly what I'm hoping for, and I'd like to learn more. First of all, how come you're interested in selling?" he inquired.

"It's far too small and too much hassle for us to deal with."

He chuckled. "You're not really selling me on that."

"I'm always straightforward. I can give you the numbers, but it's completely in the red because we don't sell the products. We simply use them internally."

"I figured that was the case. Everyone knows the LeBlanc & Broussard pralines aren't for sale."

That surprised me. "I didn't realize that was common knowledge."

"Yes, it is. Which brings me to my next question. I would like to keep using the name after buying it, if that's something you're amenable to?"

I narrowed my eyes. "That's not something I can agree on without consulting the family."

"I mainly wanted to buy it for the brand name and the recipes, of course. So I'm assuming that whoever is in charge now will hand them over to my own team. My family has been making chocolate products for over a hundred years, but our pralines are no match. "

"That's another thing I can't guarantee without talking to the team." But just imagining talking to Bailey about it felt strange, like I was betraying her in some way. Besides, I was certain that most of the recipes belonged to Celine and Isabeau. That would definitely be a difficult conversation.

"Look, man, I'll be very honest. Without a brand name or the recipes, I'd just be buying some ovens. I want to grow that business and sell these babies everywhere, make bank."

"That's a great plan."

"I know. The question is, why aren't you doing it?"

I chose my words carefully. I didn't want to lie to him, but I also didn't want to make it seem like his idea was insignificant. "Because it would still be a very small operation within the Orleans Conglomerate. And frankly, it still wouldn't be worth our time."

"Well, some of us are little fish and are happy with a mom-and-pop shop, so to speak. I'm not budging on the name and the recipes, though. That's the deal-breaker for me."

"About the name... I'm not sure that's going to work out." I didn't need to consult the family to know they wouldn't be thrilled with someone else using our name. "We don't franchise our name. And we certainly wouldn't let someone outside the family use it."

"In that case, I'm not going to be able to jump on this, but do me a favor and think about it."

"With the right marketing strategy, you could sell a lot of pralines on your own. You could communicate in your initial campaign that they *used* to be called LeBlanc & Broussard, so people make the connection. We could help with that."

"You would do that at your cost?"

I was triumphant that I still had his interest. "Yes. It might cost us a bit, but it could be worth it."

"Then I'm back in the game. I'll think about it. Thanks for the call. By the way, you said you do have some numbers you could send me?"

"Sure. Mostly about the costs."

"I want to take a look at them, although that won't be saying much without any sort of sales history. But I'm going to make some projections of my own."

"Thanks. What was your name again?"

"Ron Trudeau," he said. "You're going to have me looked up?"

"Hey, that's how I do business."

He laughed. "Don't worry, I would do the same with anyone else. But your reputation precedes you."

"Yes, the family is well-known," I agreed.

"Not just the family. You're known as being one of the most efficient and honest businesspeople in New Orleans. That's quite a reputation to have. It's why I'm even considering buying the confectionery in the first place."

The man was buttering me up—I'd been around the block enough times to know a brownnoser when I saw one—but he got points for being subtle. "I'll have my assistant send you the spreadsheets."

"We'll stay in touch," he said before hanging up.

After the conversation ended, I instructed Lydia to send him whatever he needed and then immediately called Bailey.

Surprising her wasn't fair. She'd probably need time to prepare for the ball, or maybe she even had some other plans, since she wasn't going to a different event that evening.

I debated bringing up the potential sale, but nothing was set in stone yet. There was no point upsetting her.

Chapter Nineteen
Xander

"Hi!" she answered after a couple rings. She sounded breathless.

"Am I interrupting?"

"You know me. Elbow deep in batter, keeping an eye on the oven, and so on." I liked hearing her tell me mundane things about her day. It made me feel like I was part of it. "Why are you calling?"

I couldn't believe that I'd lost track of my thoughts just because she'd told me some details. I just laughed to myself, then asked, "What are you doing on the ninth of December?"

"Is it a weekday?"

"Yeah."

"Then I'll be here."

"There's nothing on the schedule you sent me, so you don't have any delivery plans, but do you have anything going on personally?"

"I don't know. Why?" Her tone was flirty. I liked it. It was so easy to be with her and talk to her.

"Would you like to go to the LUNA Ball together?"

She gasped. "Are you serious? I would love it. Do they want pralines?"

It took me a second to realize what she meant. "I meant just us. We'll attend the ball together."

"Don't you need invitations?"

"I think they sell tickets for the public, but I actually have VIP tickets."

"And you want me to go with you?"

"Yes, I want you to be my date."

She gasped again, but it was softer this time. Then I heard a huge clang. I jumped to my feet. "Bailey, are you okay? Did you hurt yourself?"

"Damn it, I just dropped a bowl straight onto my foot! That took me by surprise."

"What? That I want to go on a date with you? We went to the restaurant on a date." Did she have a different idea of what this was than I did? Maybe I needed to be clearer, like I was when discussing business.

"I know, but this is different."

"I want to have you on my arm as my date," I assured her. "We're dating."

"Oh! Okay, I don't even really need more details. I know all about the LUNA Ball. I've always wanted to go, but somehow I have my hands full every season."

I chuckled. "That sounds unlike you, missing something Christmas related."

"Well, it's true. I've skipped one or two Christmas events over the years, especially since I started working at the confectionery."

"I haven't been to anything in years," I told her, "so this will be a long time coming for the both of us."

"This is the first year you've received invitations?"

"No, I always get them."

"And you turn them down?" she almost shrieked.

"I usually tell my assistant to just not RSVP to any of the Christmas invitations I get."

"Xander! That's a scandal. Please tell me you're joking."

"I'm not. I simply don't have time for these things."

"I bet they're mostly in the evening. You don't spend your evenings at the office, do you?"

"No," I admitted, "but I typically have better—"

"Ugh," she said, and I burst out laughing for real.

"For my own sake, I won't finish that sentence."

"You've got very good self-preservation skills. Well, I've got a mess to clean and then an outfit to visualize for the ball, so I should go."

"Sure. Can't wait."

This day was getting better and better.

After hanging up, I started to look at my to-do list in earnest. I had a lot of ground to cover and got to it. I was extremely productive until about three o'clock when my phone rang. Isabeau. I usually didn't like answering phone calls during work hours unless it was absolutely necessary, but my grandmothers were always the exception.

"Hello," I said enthusiastically.

"Hi, Xander darling. Am I interrupting anything?"

"No, or I wouldn't have answered."

"Yes, that's true."

"Can I help you with anything?"

"I was wondering if you've made a decision yet about the confectionery."

I frowned, leaning back in my chair. Then I got up, stretching my legs a bit as I walked through the office. "No. I told you I wouldn't decide until after Christmas."

"But I'm sure you're already leaning one way or the other."

"No, I'm not." I put a hand in my pocket, looking outside. Even from this floor, I could still see the Christmas decorations throughout the city. I made a mental note to bring Bailey here. She'd absolutely love it.

"Right," she said.

"Isabeau, what is it? It's not like you to call under pretense."

"Who says I did?"

"I do." After a bit, I added, "Am I wrong?"

"No. My real question was what's happening with Bailey?"

Nothing could've shocked me more.

"Let's start another way. What do you know?"

"Xander, that's not how this works."

"I'm a grown-ass man, Isabeau—sorry for the language. You don't get to just question me about relationship matters."

"I usually wouldn't. You know for a fact that I've never asked what you do with your personal life."

"That's right."

"But I care about Bailey."

That shocked me yet again. "Okaaay," I said.

"She and her sister have been doing marvelously with the confectionery over the years. I don't know who else would give that business such love and devotion. I'm very fond of Avery and Bailey, and I wouldn't want them to get hurt."

I realized a split second later that my own grandmother was warning me. "I don't plan to hurt either of them."

"Sometimes in business decisions, you have collateral damage. And now you're mixing business with personal, as far as I've heard."

"Which comes back to my question. What do you know?" She was fishing for information. Someone must have told her something.

"I knew something was going on at the open house. She was red in the face half the evening, and it was definitely not from the nonalcoholic eggnog. You two were constantly looking at each other throughout the event. I kept waiting for someone to tell me what was going on."

"And now you've lost your patience." I finally understood.

"I wanted to be sure, but I couldn't be. And I wanted to have this conversation with you. Bailey is a wonderful woman, but if you plan to go ahead with a sale or closing down the operation, then be careful not to hurt her. She cares a lot about the business."

"I know."

"How do you feel about Bailey?"

I scoffed. "Way to put me on the spot."

"You and I are very much alike, Xander. We call things like we see them."

"True." A trait I was passing on to Bella. It was one of my finest achievements. "I don't actually know how to answer that."

It was the truth.

"This is wonderful," Isabeau exclaimed.

I frowned. "Did you hear what I just said?" Maybe she'd misunderstood.

"Yes. This is so unlike you. Oh, Xander, you're young, and I can't possibly explain to you."

Ah, now I get it. There was the reasonable side to Isabeau, and then there was the other side, the one that insisted her perfumes had powers. I had an inkling that the other side had come out for this call.

"Some things in life aren't straightforward," she continued. "You can't see where the path ends unless you actually walk down it. Anyway, I won't keep bothering you. I'm sure you've got a million things to do, and I've got all the information I need."

That was alarming because I hadn't really shared much with her.

"Isabeau, are you sure you're not imagining things?" I double-checked.

"Xander, don't insult me. When have I ever done that?"

That was a fair question. The answer was never, but still...

"Right. Have a great day, Isabeau."

"And you."

After we finished talking, I played our conversation over in my mind. I still couldn't really tell what she was so excited about. But Isabeau and Celine had their own unique ways of looking at things. One of these days, maybe I'd understand their point of view, but today was not the day.

Chapter Twenty

Bailey

Even though I had my hands full the entire week, I'd been googling the LUNA Ball every chance I got. I'd mostly found pictures of models, which wasn't very helpful, as I wanted to see what the guests were wearing, but it didn't matter. I had a few amazing dresses and planned to bring my favorite one out to play. Oh, I was so excited.

Bailey, focus. You've still got deliveries to do today, and you don't want to get your addresses mixed up.

That wasn't really possible, though, as I only had two, and both were in the French Quarter. One was Julian's bar, a place I really enjoyed delivering to. I was surprised the first year I'd seen the bar on the list, but Julian himself had assured me that our pralines were a big draw during the Christmas season. People specifically came for the pralines at Christmastime, not for the Sazerac, as usual.

The other delivery was at Isabeau and Celine's fragrance shop.

"This is strange. They've never asked for a delivery," I told Avery.

"Isabeau called me this morning and said they're dying for some pralines. I figured since you'll be in the Quarter anyway, you can take some to them. Do you mind? I can do it if it's too much."

"I was just surprised, that's all. Did she tell you what she wants?"

"No, and I didn't have time to ask."

"Don't worry. I will."

Since I was on a break anyway, I decided to do it right now. I was done with the batter and only had to wrap up the batch that was currently cooling. I made a mental note of everything we had. We did have their cherry favorites, but not the pistachio.

I hesitated for a split second. In the past, I'd never had any qualms about calling Isabeau. *But you weren't sleeping with her grandson back then,* a voice said in the back of my mind. That was the crux of it. But Isabeau was oblivious to that, and this was simply about pralines. I'd talked to her about them a million times. I was pleased when she answered.

"Bailey, my girl, nice to hear from you."

"Hey, Isabeau. My sister tells me you're in the mood for some pralines."

"We've been craving them for quite some time, but we didn't want to bust into anyone else's stash."

That made me laugh. "Don't worry, I've got you covered. We have cherry pralines but no pistachios. What else do you want? There is nougat, too, and strawberry."

"Just mix and match. It doesn't even matter."

Doesn't even matter? That was unlike Isabeau. She usually had very specific requests for her pralines, and she'd once explained why: "If I take on calories, I intend to make every single one count."

"Then I'll just make you a nice mix. How long are you at the shop?"

"We don't close very early. It's best if you come after you drop by Julian's."

Now I was downright suspicious. She sounded sneaky, but I knew Isabeau well enough to realize that I wasn't going to get to the bottom of this anytime soon.

"I'll see you later, then."

"Sure. Can't wait."

I didn't have too much time to mull it over, as I needed to start packing the cooled pralines. The next batch would have to wait until tomorrow morning. Or maybe Avery could wrap them before leaving.

My sister popped into the kitchen just as I finished packing up everything. "Need help bringing this to the car?"

"I'm good. They're not so heavy. If you can get to those this evening, that's fine." I pointed to the tray that was still cooling. "If not, I'll do them in the morning."

"I'll take care of it. You spoke to Isabeau?"

"Yeah."

"She sounded a bit odd when she called me this morning," Avery said.

"I had that same feeling when I spoke to her just now."

She grinned. "I guess you're going to find out soon enough what it's about."

"Exactly. Bye, sis. See you tomorrow."

I quickly finished the first errand in the Quarter. I was surprised that Julian wasn't at the bar. He'd always been there for previous deliveries.

As I walked to Celine and Isabeau's shop on Dumaine, I smiled at the slightest hint of music in the air, remembering my dance with Xander. I schooled my features when I arrived in front of Fragrant Delights.

I'd only been here twice before, but the shop was just as quaint and gorgeous as I remembered. They'd changed the Christmas decorations this year. They used to have a set of old-fashioned candles, with actual flames, placed strategically in the window, but now they had garlands of twinkle lights. I liked both, but the lights completely fit their shop. Besides, it was safer.

When I walked in, I was surprised to see that they were completely alone. I looked at the business hours written on the door. They'd already closed half an hour ago.

"Hi, Bailey," Celine greeted me. "Thank you so much for coming with pralines. We've been in the mood for them for days."

She immediately took the boxes and carried them to the counter. She and Isabeau each opened one.

"I can always bring more."

"Don't be silly. This is a dangerous season anyway," Isabeau said. "I keep finding goodies left and right. If I had more of your pralines on hand, goodness, who knows what might happen."

The two of them looked at each other after they'd each munched on their third praline. Then Celine turned to me. "We have something for you. I hope we're not overstepping boundaries."

"What is it?" I asked.

"You know that we love making custom perfumes," Isabeau said. "We took the liberty of creating one for you."

"That's so thoughtful of you, but you really didn't have to."

Isabeau lowered herself a bit and took something from under the counter. "Think of it as an early Christmas present, if nothing else, and if you don't like it, we'll make a new one."

I'd never do that on principle. Even if I hated it—which I very much doubted—I'd politely thank them.

Celine opened a small bottle and held it out for me. I leaned in, inhaling deeply.

"This is perfect." I was stunned. I couldn't even describe how I knew it was perfect, but it simply was. "What notes are there?"

"A mix: bergamot, orange, lilac, freesia, a bit of peach."

"It's just... it's me."

I couldn't get over my own surprise. I immediately put some on my wrists and sniffed it. The notes blended with my skin, and it smelled even better than directly from the bottle.

The two of them grinned at me with a cat-that-got-the-canary expression. I had that feeling from the phone call again, that they were being sneaky. But for the life of me, I couldn't figure it out. It didn't even matter.

Lowering my hand, I asked, "How much does it cost?"

Celine jerked her head back. "Nothing! It's a gift, dear."

"We've waited far too long to give you a perfume if you ask me," Isabeau added.

And yet they didn't have one for Avery, which made me even more suspicious. But I wasn't going to look a gift horse in the mouth.

"Thanks so much."

"All the hard work you do over the holidays—well, all year long, really—we just wanted to make sure you knew how special you are."

"Thank you. I'll cherish this."

I felt like something was up for sure. In order to stop my suspicious mind, I looked around the shop. It had such a fantastic feel to it. Almost supernatural, like if an otherworldly creature popped up in a corner, it would simply belong here. The floor-to-ceiling shelves were filled with small bottles and crystals. I understood why they liked spending their whole day here. It felt like a safe place.

"By the way," Celine said, "how has Xander been treating you and Avery?"

I instantly spun around, feeling like I was at school and the teacher just caught me cheating on my exam.

"He's... He's been c-civil." Great, now I was stammering.

Celine looked at me intently. Isabeau was a bit stone-faced, which was unlike her. I had the eerie feeling that she was trying very hard to keep a poker face.

"So, he's not being too hard on you or too demanding?" Celine went on.

"No. Not at all."

"We've heard rumors that he's been showing up in quite a few places where you're making deliveries," Isabeau said. She'd never sounded stranger than now. I'd definitely been right in my assumptions.

"I think that's a good thing. Gives him a chance to see that charities count on us and that we make people happy. Maybe it'll soften him up."

"Hmm," Isabeau said. "If he does give you grief, let us know."

"Really? What will you do?"

"Sort everything out, of course," Celine replied.

Now it was my turn to fight to keep a straight face. These two were a force to be reckoned with. But so was Xander. I knew Isabeau could single-handedly order half the French Quarter around to do her bidding, but not him.

"It's been great seeing you two. Thank you again for the perfume."

"Thank you for the pralines," Isabeau said.

I had an inkling that they'd just been a ruse to get me here, but why? For the perfume? That seemed strange, even for them. But I knew just where I was going to wear this exclusive perfume the first time: at the LUNA Ball with Xander.

CHAPTER TWENTY-ONE
BAILEY

On Friday evening, I was over the moon. I kept looking at myself in the full-length mirror on the back of my bathroom door. I was very happy with my outfit. My dress was black with gold accents running off in waves all around the fabric. If I twirled, it shimmered nicely. I'd pair it with gold shoes, of course, and I was going to wear my favorite coat again. It was elegant and classy and complemented everything.

I'd used a straightener on my hair, and Lee Stafford Heat Protection Shine Mist. It was my absolute favorite hair product, and it gave my thick hair a very glamorous shimmer. I was so ready for this evening. My makeup was a little more extravagant than usual, with smoky eyes—heavy on the mascara. My lips were nude, though, not just because I didn't want to overdo it but because I foresaw the opportunity for kissing and didn't want to let my lipstick get in the way. And my ultimate accessory? The perfume from Isabeau and Celine. I applied some on my wrists, behind my ears, and—because I felt extra naughty—between my breasts.

I shimmied, looking at myself in the mirror. I was so ready. This was shaping up to be one of the best Christmas seasons.

Xander was picking me up, and I was a bit more nervous than last time. I still wasn't sure if I should've told Celine and Isabeau that he and I were seeing each other, but it felt like it wasn't my place. Xander should have that conversation with his grandmothers.

When the doorbell rang, I yelled, "It's open," but nothing happened.

Oh crap. He probably can't hear me from the other side of the door and past my carols.

I was laughing at myself as I hurried to the door and opened it with a grin. "Come in. Actually, you know what? You don't even have to. I'm ready."

He smiled at me, his eyes crinkling at the corners. "You look stunning."

"Thank you. Let me just turn off the music." I grabbed my phone and bag, which I'd strategically placed next to the entrance with my coat. "Now I'm truly ready."

"You're happy," he remarked.

"Of course. Christmas is approaching, and I'm attending the LUNA Ball for the first time ever with the sexiest man in New Orleans. How could I not be happy?"

He pulled me close to him, his eyes darkening. "You smell absolutely delicious."

"Yes, I forgot to tell you. This week I went to your grandmothers' store."

Xander stopped in the act of buttoning my coat and looked up at me. "Go on."

"It was a bit bizarre." Maybe he could tell me what was going on, as I still wasn't quite sure. "They called Avery out of the blue to say they were in the mood for pralines, and then when I asked which ones they wanted, Isabeau insisted that it didn't matter. And when it comes to your grandmothers—"

"It always matters," the two of us said together.

"Exactly. Anyway, when I showed up at the shop, they had this custom-made perfume for me. Let me tell you, it's perfect. I. Love. It! But the whole thing still felt a bit strange."

The corner of Xander's mouth twitched upward, and he shook his head.

"You know what's going on?" I asked.

"I have an idea."

"Can you fill me in? Because I'm starting to feel like I'm missing something."

He sighed, still looking amused as we walked outside. I closed the door behind me, locking it up, and buttoned the rest of my coat.

"Did they tell you what it contains?"

"Bergamot, orange, lilac, freesia, and peach, I think."

He nodded triumphantly. "They have a whole story behind lilac. They believe it's responsible for my parents getting together."

"Oh, I see." I laughed, but then panic started to crawl up my neck. "Wait. Does that mean they know? Because they asked if you've been giving me any trouble."

"I'll tell you more in the car."

"There *is* more to it?" I was panicking even more. "I played it off as if there was nothing going on between us."

"Bailey, relax," he said into my ear just before he opened my door.

"I can't. It feels like I've been lying to them."

He kissed my hand and pushed my legs into the car before closing the door.

Oh, this man! He was so infuriating. Why wasn't he just telling me what was going on?

Once he got in the car, he said, "Don't worry about anything. My grandmothers adore you. And they totally know what's going on."

I groaned. "How will I face them the next time?"

"With your head held high."

"How do you know that they know?" Was I even making sense? I wasn't sure anymore, but the guilt was eating me up. I looked up to Isabeau and Celine immensely. They'd been a huge influence in my life, and I didn't want to let them down.

"Because Isabeau called me and, in no uncertain terms, told me that she's very fond of you and doesn't want me to hurt you."

I was too stunned to reply, so I just stared silently out the windshield.

Xander glanced over at me as we sped through the city. "Bailey, you okay?"

"She actually said that? That she cares that much about me?"

"Yeah."

"I appreciate that she's looking out for me. But why didn't they say anything to me when I was at the shop?"

"My guess? They didn't want to put you on the spot. In any case, I'm the one who needs to talk to them."

I swallowed hard and looked at him. "And you aren't mad?"

"Why would I be?"

"I don't know. That your own grandmothers gave you 'the talk.'"

"Nah, it's all good," Xander said.

"What did you tell her when she lectured you?"

When we stopped at a red light, he turned and looked straight at me. "That I don't plan to hurt you, not in a million years. And that she's not getting more information from me anytime soon."

I laughed, pinching his shoulder. "I bet that went over well."

"She was a bit surprised, hence why she probably tried to get the details out of you."

I beamed at him, starting to relax. I could finally focus on the party again. "I'm so excited about tonight."

"So am I."

We arrived a little while later, and I was awed by the sight before me. I'd seen photos of the LUNA Ball over the years, so some of it was familiar: the extravagant designs of the outfits, the lighting devices, the general vibe. The VIP area was amazing. It was quite far away from the main event, in a separate room that was lavishly decorated with velvet couches and silver candleholders.

The Christmas decor was discreet but festive. They'd hung mistletoe here and there, and there was a small but perfectly decorated tree in the center of the room, with a string of lights in the shape of presents all around it. I planned to steal that idea.

Xander and I had watched the fashion show for a while from outside the VIP room, where there was a wide berth reserved only for VIP guests. But once we smelled food, we both decided to come in here. I was currently eating my third portion of cake. My appetizer and main course were also cake. They had several, and I'd made it my mission to try all of them by the end of the evening. Naturally, that meant I didn't have room to eat anything else.

"Do I see more cake?" Xander asked, coming up in front of me.

"Guilty. Have you seen how many they have? I need to try all of them. Don't you want any?"

"I'm not really a sweets man."

I gasped a bit theatrically. "You can't say that to someone who makes pralines all day long. It's a sacrilege."

"I do like your pralines."

"That's right. Butter me up."

Xander grinned and then brushed his fingers over my cheek. "You've got some powdered sugar there."

"How did it end up on my cheek?" Then again, it wasn't really a huge surprise with the large bites I'd taken.

"Are you having fun?"

I nodded feverishly. "Yes. This whole place has such dreamy vibes. I especially love the idea of the string of lights in the shape of gift boxes."

"Huh?" I pointed to the tree. "Oh, right. Yeah, it does look good."

"You didn't even notice it until now?"

"On a scale of one to ten, do you want the truth?"

"Always."

He leaned in, whispering in my ear, "I didn't even notice the tree."

"Xander, that can't possibly be true."

"I'm not noticing much tonight. Only you."

My breath hitched as butterflies roamed around in my stomach. This man definitely knew how to sweet-talk me.

"Xander LeBlanc, what an honor to have you at this event," a man said, walking up to us.

Xander instantly straightened up, turning to him. "Danielson, good to see you."

Danielson then looked at me. "And you are?"

"This is Bailey LeCarre," Xander said, "My date tonight."

I swear to God, my chest pushed itself forward all on its own, simply bursting with pride at his words.

"It's an amazing event. I love it," I gushed.

"I can't really take credit for much except sponsoring some of it." He touched my arm. "But I'm guessing you're the one I need to thank for Xander being here."

"Oh, well—"

"Definitely yes," Xander said. "I came because I knew Bailey would enjoy herself."

"Well, since you're here, I'd like to steal you away for a few moments if I can," Danielson said.

Xander looked at me. He was truly deferring this to me? Would he turn him down if I said no? That was silly. Why would I even do that? "Sure. I'll taste more of that amazing cake."

Both of them started to laugh, then went a few steps outside the room.

I'd said that statement in jest, but looking at my plate, the remaining piece of cake did look terribly lonely. It needed a friend. So, I went back to the table with the sweets. They had food as well—mostly canapés, which made sense. You didn't want a room like this to smell like jambalaya or something like that.

I decided on a chocolate cake. Just as I added a slice to my plate, I felt Xander put a hand on my waist and looked up, surprised he'd returned so quickly. Only this sexy man could distract me from cake.

"Xander LeBlanc," a voice said from behind us, as we both turned around.

"Thomas!" Xander exclaimed.

The man named Thomas seemed to be the same age as us. He shook Xander's hand. "Haven't seen you in a while, man."

Xander gestured to me. "Bailey, this is an old friend from high school, Thomas Halsey. Thomas, this is my girlfriend, Bailey."

I loved how that sounded. *Girlfriend.*

"Nice to meet you, Bailey, and congratulations for getting this one here tonight. When I heard you were attending, I thought some miracle must have happened to pull Xander LeBlanc out of his office. Now things are starting to make sense."

Xander shrugged. "It's a busy season."

"I know, man, but even so... Anyway, I'm not complaining. If it weren't for you, my family and I would be in huge financial issues. We almost bought into Kyle and Beau Deveraux's scheme. I know many who did and handed them money."

Xander scoffed. "Too many, unfortunately. But I wasn't going to let them do any more harm."

"They were always assholes," Thomas said, shaking his head. "Even in high school. Don't know how they turned out like that. Their parents are decent people. I've dealt with them a few times. Their sister, Grace, is nothing like them either."

"I've met the parents a few times but never had the pleasure of meeting the sister. The good thing is that they won't be harming anyone again anytime soon."

"No, they won't. No one's heard from them in months," Thomas said. Then he looked at me apologetically. "Sorry for interrupting your evening with unpleasant talk. Enjoy the party. I'll see you around."

After he left, I looked at Xander inquisitively. "What was that exactly?"

He schooled his features. "Georgie actually dated Kyle way before Julian, and he was being very uncivil toward her. He was even badmouthing her to clients. I helped my brother remove him from her life. Then again, Kyle and Beau made it easy for us. They stole money from a lot of businesspeople in the city. Long story, but it's over now."

"So, you stepped in to save your family, huh?" I teased.

"Of course," he said without hesitation.

Oh, this man. "I like that you can be ruthless for a good cause."

Xander jerked his head back. "I don't believe anyone has ever said that before."

"It's true. If you think something will benefit your family, you don't have any qualms, do you?"

"That's right. Family first, always."

And I melted. That kind of loyalty was hard to find nowadays.

"See, ruthless for a good cause. And sometimes just ruthless."

He frowned. "Hey, what do you mean? What do you base that on?"

"The fact that one, you're very Grinch-y when it comes to Christmas." I started counting on my fingers. "Two, you don't like sweets. There is something seriously wrong with that. My mom has a saying that you can eat dessert even when you don't have any more space left because dessert goes directly into the heart." I put a hand on his chest.

"And third?"

"Hmm. I forgot."

Xander tilted closer, and I heard a low growl reverberate in his chest. I felt it under my palm too. "Keep talking like that and I'll throw you over my shoulder, take you out of here, and then we can go through all of those points again. Alone."

"What difference would that make?" I asked, then realized what he meant a second later. "Oh, you think you can convince me otherwise with sexy times? Hmmm... that's not really how it works. I mean, you do get major kudos for your prowess in bed. But it doesn't negate my points."

I felt another growl beneath my palm. Damn, I was enjoying this. I couldn't believe I was riling him up so easily. It was fun, and I wondered how far I could push it.

But I didn't get a chance to find out because we were interrupted by yet another person who was amazed that Xander was here and needed to talk to him.

The same episode repeated a few more times, which made me realize that word was traveling around.

I would've expected my Grinch-y guy to make excuses, but I was surprised by his social skills. Although he disliked such events, he made small talk with everyone before proceeding to more detailed business questions. I couldn't get over how proudly he presented me as his date every time.

As the evening went by, I started to sit down more. I chose the couch closest to the Christmas tree so I could admire all the ornaments.

"Are you feeling okay?" Xander asked, and I startled because I hadn't realized he'd taken a seat next to me. He'd been across the room when I checked a few minutes ago.

"Just a bit tired."

"Want us to call it a night?"

"Did you finish your conversation with that finance guy?"

"Bailey, I came here for you. If you're ready to go, then we'll leave."

How could he say things like that? "Well, I've had my fill of cake."

"How many slices did you end up having?" he asked with a grin.

"Five." I cleared my throat. "Okay, seven. But they were little! You saw how small they are."

Xander just smiled. "Do you have a favorite?"

"I can't say anything definitive because they do have a few more kinds. I just have no room left."

"Well, if you're ready, we can go."

We rose from the couch at the same time. The main room was still fairly crowded. We didn't bid goodbye to anyone but the host, thanking him for throwing the event.

"What are we doing now?" I asked Xander.

"I believe I promised you a fire in my penthouse."

"Yes, yes, yes! I've been looking forward to your fireplace."

He brought his mouth to my ear as we left the venue. "And I've been looking forward to having you at my place."

Chapter Twenty-Two
Xander

It didn't take us long to arrive in the business district. I lived in a modern building, and one of the amenities I appreciated most besides the concierge was the underground parking.

Bailey looked around as we rode the elevator.

"Why are you so quiet?" I asked her.

"I've always wondered what it's like to live in one of these buildings."

"What's the verdict?"

"Judging by the parking lot and the elevator, I like it so far. I truly love modern structures."

"Wait till you see the penthouse."

The doors of the elevator opened a short while later, and we stepped out on the top floor. I unlocked the door to the penthouse with my fingerprint.

"I like that too," Bailey said. "Very safe." Then she giggled. "Very Bond, James Bond."

As I opened the door, the lights inside turned on one by one.

The entire place was mostly one huge open space. The bedroom was separate, as was my office, but the living and kitchen areas were merged.

"This place suits you," she murmured.

"What do you mean? Heartless?"

"Hey, I said you're a Grinch, not that you don't have a heart. There's a huge difference. What I meant is that it seems very efficient. Very streamlined. I really like it."

"Does that mean you like me too?"

She looked at me, narrowing her eyes. "Not sure. I might decide after tonight, depending on..."

I wiggled my eyebrows. "My prowess in bed?"

"I was going to say how good your fire was, but that works too."

We left our coats and shoes by the entrance, then went into the living room. I led her directly to the couch, which faced the fireplace.

Her eyes sparkled. "This is my favorite fireplace ever." It was in the middle of the room, encircled by glass, so no matter where you sat, you had a view of the fire. "It looks completely unused."

"I only light a fire if Bella comes here because she enjoys it so much. Or if I'm having family over."

I'd already put the wood and the lighter by the fireplace.

"You thought you had it all in the bag already, huh?" she asked as I lowered myself in front of it and opened the door.

"What do you mean?" I asked when she motioned to the stuff I'd set out.

"You were so sure I was coming home with you tonight."

"I knew the fireplace would be a big draw." I wiggled my eyebrows and got her to laugh.

"Do you want me to help?"

"No, I'll only need a few minutes. Then we can watch it burn from the couch."

"Right, then, I'll await you there."

I held the door open for a bit until the fire was drawing properly. Before closing it, it dimmed a little, but not too much, and I knew it was good.

"This looks really lovely," Bailey said. "I love it."

She was curled up on the couch with her feet up next to her. I sat down on her other side and took her hand in mine.

"I'm glad you like it. So... was it worth the trip here?"

"Definitely. You looked so manly starting the fire." She brought her mouth to my ear. "It sort of fired me up too."

Oh, I definitely didn't need to hear that. I was already fighting all my urges. I'd wanted to take that dress off her ever since I first saw her tonight, and even more so once we stepped in here and there was no one else to bother us. But I wanted her to enjoy the fire first before I devoured her.

"You're awfully silent. I'm starting to get suspicious," she teased.

"Good, you should."

"I see. You're having sexy thoughts, huh?"

"Woman, can you read my mind?"

She leaned in even closer to me. I felt the shape of her full breasts against my arm. I was sporting a hard-on already.

"No, but coincidentally, that's where my mind went too. I swear this fire is giving me strange ideas. It's like an aphrodisiac or something. Or maybe it's all these muscles."

She grazed her fingertips over my chest and then lowered her hand down my abs. But I had another idea. She could enjoy the fire while I was buried deep inside her. One thing didn't exclude the other.

I moved slightly so I could use both hands and then grabbed her ass, pulling her into my lap. She yelped before starting to laugh.

"Easy there. What are you trying to...? Oh, this is what you're doing."

I settled her right over my cock.

"I'm *so* on board with this."

I lifted her ass a bit so I could drag her dress past it, then cinched it up her waist. For a split second, I thought she wasn't wearing lingerie at all, and I nearly came just at the thought. Then I realized she was wearing panties that were skin-colored.

I groaned at the sight.

"I bet you thought I was naked, huh? That's the point." She got down from my lap and immediately pushed them to her feet. "It's better to get them out of the way," she whispered, then climbed back on my lap.

I opened the buckle of my belt, needing to relieve some of the pressure. I couldn't believe I was so on edge already.

"Turn around," I said.

"Why?"

"So you can watch the fire."

Her eyes glinted for a split second, and then she did as I said. I lowered my zipper, the sight of her bare ass above me making me even harder than before. Holding her waist with my left hand, I pushed my pants under my ass with the right one. Not a lot, just enough to free my cock. Then I simply left it between us while I grabbed her dress.

"Where's the zipper?" I almost couldn't recognize my voice. I was blind with need, driven by this insane urgency to be one with this woman.

She pointed to her back. "Here." Her voice sounded off too.

I lowered the zipper before yanking the dress over her head. She took care of her own bra before I even reached for it. As soon as it was on the floor, I cupped her breasts and pulled her toward me so her back was flat against my chest.

"Enjoy the fire, beautiful."

"Like this?"

"Yes, like this. You enjoy the fire, and I'll fuck you so good. You'll like it, I promise. Just relax against me."

I knew it wasn't really possible, though, because her body was already taut, anticipating pleasure. I caressed her breasts, teasing them with my fingers. Then I flicked both nipples at the same time with my thumbs. I looked into the fire, too, but I was focusing on her body's reactions more. Her stomach was rising and falling with quick breaths. When her breath hitched, I lowered one hand slowly over her, between her breasts to her navel, and then passed it to her pussy. I only teased her folds with my forefinger and middle finger, moving them up and down at a lazy pace. My cock felt like it was about to explode, hanging between us, hard as fuck. I pushed her farther up a bit so I could kiss her neck and shoulders. She looked down at my hand between her legs.

"The fire. Keep looking at the fire," I instructed.

"Okay. But don't stop. Please."

"I wasn't planning to, beautiful."

I wanted to tease her, but I wasn't cruel. She didn't just need teasing, she needed a bit of pleasure too. I pressed three fingers to her clit, circling it with just the slightest bit of pressure.

"Xander, Xander, Xander," she chanted, then abruptly rose onto her knees as if a current shot right through her. Then she sat back down, hovering over my cock.

This time, her folds grazed right over the length of my erection. A groan tore from my chest.

"Xander," she whispered again. "Please... please, I want this."

"What do you want, beautiful?"

"You."

"I want you to be more specific. You want my cock, or you want to come?"

"Both. I want to come, but I want your cock inside me."

Hearing her say this dissolved my last thread of self-restraint. I grabbed her hips with both hands, positioning her where I needed her, and thrust inside her as she gasped and looked over her shoulder.

"Keep looking at the fire, babe. Just feel what I'm doing to you."

"I'll do whatever you say, just don't stop. Please."

Her words fueled me like nothing else. I moved her up and down the length of my cock. Watching her ass cheeks mold over my thighs every time was downright exquisite. But this wasn't enough—there was no way for me to move in this position. I quickly assessed my options. I wanted her to face the fire, which only left me with one.

I moved her off me, and she cried out. "Xander, please..."

"Get on your knees on the carpet." It was thick and soft enough that she wouldn't get rug burn.

She immediately dropped to all fours, legs wide, pushing her ass backward, already wanting me to thrust into her. I wasn't going to make her wait any longer. I positioned myself behind her and slid in all the way. When I was inside her to the hilt, a current of pleasure rocked my entire body. This was going to be more powerful than anything I'd ever experienced. The connection I had to this woman was hard to describe, but I was eager to strengthen it.

I moved back and then slammed inside her even harder. Bailey was moving, too, pushing her ass back and forth, meeting my rhythm. I paused every few seconds, kissing her back, especially when she curled up. She was on the edge, but I wanted a better angle, and I needed to feel closer to her.

"Rise up, Bailey. Onto your knees."

"What do you mean?" she whispered.

I leaned forward, putting my hands on her rib cage, and then pulled her lightly to me. She moved easily, going soft in my arms as I straightened her up.

"Oh my God." She was once again with her back flat against my chest.

"Are you comfortable like this?"

"Yes. I feel you so deep. It's surreal."

I liked this position even more—I could touch her breasts and her clit, feel every vibration of her body as I pushed in and out. My movements weren't desperate anymore. They were precise, deep, and slow. Even though I was desperate to climax and to bring her pleasure, I knew it would be much more intense like this. I moved my hand aimlessly from her belly to her breasts, resting on her rib cage a few times. I could feel every trepidation in her breath, every time she was too overwhelmed by the sensations.

"Xandeeer!" Her pussy spasmed.

I put one hand to her clit, flicking it with as little pressure as possible. This was heightening everything for her. She dropped her head on my shoulder, closing her eyes.

"I didn't say you could stop watching the fire, Bailey."

Gasping, she opened her eyes again and straightened, looking at the fire as if it was all she could do.

"What do you feel, baby? Tell me."

"My pussy will explode. I can't even."

"Do you want me to move faster? Do you want me to let you come?"

"Yes, please, right now. Yes." Her voice shook and then broke completely on that one syllable.

I pressed my fingers on her clit while I drove deep inside her. She cried out instantly, and then her body went completely rigid. She dropped her hands by her sides and her head back on my shoulder. This time I didn't say anything, just watched her succumb to the pleasure, giving in to it completely. The rhythmic squeezing of her pussy drove me insane. I couldn't postpone my own climax any longer. I moved faster, thrusting deeper.

"I need you on all fours, gorgeous. Right now."

"Whatever you need, Xander. Anything." She planted her palms on the floor. I rested one hand on the middle of her back, the other on her clit. She was still so sensitive.

"I want to make you come again right now, while I'm still buried inside you, before I let go."

She came the next second. The force of her orgasm shocked me completely. She'd come so beautifully only seconds ago that I didn't think she could come so powerfully again, but I'd been wrong. She cried out, and her elbows gave in. She lowered her shoulders before straightening them up again, as if a current had gone through her, and threw her head back.

Watching her let go a second time sent me right over the edge. My climax was just as powerful as hers. I couldn't stop it if I wanted to, and fuck if I did. I wanted to freeze this moment in time so it would never end.

"Babe, you feel so damn good." I no longer followed a rhythm, just let my body take over, doing whatever it needed in order to ride out the pleasure. It seemed never-ending. She was still crying out; I knew this was just as intense for her and just as surprising.

My climax wound down almost at the same time hers did. I made myself push until she felt soft under my hands. The change was subtle, but I couldn't possibly miss it. Her muscles relaxed everywhere in her body.

"Xander," she whispered as I pulled out. She curled up on the carpet, tucking her feet under her.

"Babe, are you comfortable?"

She glanced at the fire. "I'm trying to memorize everything about this moment. It's perfect," she whispered in a lower tone, as if afraid I might hear her. But I wanted her to know that I was right there with her, so I brought my mouth to her ear.

"I know. It's the same for me." When I moved back slightly, I noticed she was watching me with wide eyes.

"Really?"

"Yeah." I took one of the blankets from the couch and put it over her.

"I'm not cold, but this is cozy. I think I could even fall asleep here."

"I'll carry you to bed."

"And miss the fire?" She seemed suspiciously alert all of a sudden, as if she'd just remembered the fire.

"It is, of course, the main attraction."

She playfully narrowed her eyes. "Well, that depends..."

"Still need time to decide which one is your favorite?"

"Maybe. But you're so smart, having your way with me in front of the fire. That makes it very hard for me to make up my mind."

"Is that so?"

"You win, but only by a very slight margin."

I smirked. "The night is young, I might convince you yet that I deserve to win by a very, very large margin."

Chapter Twenty-Three

Xander

"Fucking hell, everyone is incompetent today," I exclaimed on Friday evening, one week after having Bailey at my house. I'd been on edge ever since, wanting more and more of her. My temperament was insufferable.

My assistant poked her head in. "Xander, I heard you talking. Do you need something?"

"No, I was just talking to myself. Everyone sent me spreadsheets done incorrectly today. Three different people. What are the odds?"

She looked like she was about to burst out laughing.

"You know something, Lydia?"

"It might be because it's Friday afternoon and a week away from Christmas." She smiled apologetically. "I don't think people are taking work too seriously."

"Things still need to get done."

"Well, I was actually about to tell you that I'm gone for the day unless you need something from me."

It was on the tip of my tongue to say, "It's not even that late yet," but then I noticed the time. It was five o'clock.

"Sure, have a great weekend."

"You, too, Xander." She started to leave and then turned around. "Um. Maybe a word of advice..."

"You know I'm always open to advice."

"Don't call or send people any more emails tonight. You'll just get more frustrated. I really don't think anyone else, even in the Orleans Conglomerate, is working."

I couldn't argue with that, because I'd sent three emails in the past half hour and didn't get a single reply. Who stopped working at four thirty on a Friday?

I could only imagine what Bailey would have to say about it. Just thinking about her made me laugh at myself. She might have a point. I truly was a fucking Grinch, and I never thought I'd say that about myself. It was the last Friday before Christmas. Of course people probably had other things to do.

In fact, I no longer wanted to stay at the office either. Those spreadsheets needed fixing, but not tonight.

Speaking of spreadsheets, I opened the one Bailey sent me with her schedule. Bingo. I knew she had an event tonight. The note only said "children's hospital," but there was no hour listed, just "afternoon." I was babysitting Bella, but only later, at eight o'clock. I wondered if Bailey was still there, and I decided to call her. She answered after five rings.

"Hey," she whispered.

"Hi, Bailey."

"Listen, I'm at the—"

"Children's hospital," I finished for her.

"How do you...? Oh, the spreadsheet."

"Are you going to be there for long?"

"Yes. Tim is actually reading to us from his favorite storybook. It's going to take a while until we make the rounds."

"Mind if I join you?"

"At the hospital?"

"Yes. You're delivering pralines to the kids, right?"

"Yes, and the staff."

"Could you use another pair of hands?"

"Definitely." She sounded relieved. "It's only me and Avery tonight. Gustav was supposed to come, too, but he was coming down with a cold, and

I didn't want him to get anyone sick. But wait, aren't you spending the evening with Bella?"

"Later. I'll be there as soon as possible. Where can I find you?"

"Just text me when you're here. I don't know if we'll have moved on by then."

"Sure."

As soon as I hung up, I grabbed my coat and headed down to my car, aiming to get the children's hospital as quickly as possible.

Another crazy thing about the last Friday before Christmas? Traffic. It took me a whole fucking forty-five minutes to get there. I kept texting Bailey on the way, and she assured me that they were still there. Just as I arrived, she told me they'd moved on to the second floor, and I went straight there.

When I stepped on the second level, I heard Bailey's and Avery's voices coming from one of the rooms. Following the sound, I stepped inside a room with five kids. Three had their parents next to them, but two were alone. Bailey was sitting on one of their beds, Avery on the other one.

"You're here," Bailey said, smiling at me. "We were just telling stories about you."

"Yeah, you're Mr. Grinch," the boy next to Bailey said. He looked pale and had dark circles under his eyes.

"The Grinch who stole Christmas," another one of the kids said.

Ordinarily, I'd pretend to at least be mad about this, but these kids seemed to enjoy meeting the Grinch.

"Yep. Here I am, the Grinch at your disposal. How might I ruin Christmas this year?"

Bailey's eyes flew open. Even Avery gave me an appreciative smile. I had no idea where that came from, but clearly it did the trick, because all the kids were clapping and laughing.

"We've never met the Grinch before. Please don't steal Christmas this year, please, please," a girl said. "I need it more than ever. I told Santa to bring Mom and Dad some money so we can pay for the food."

My whole body felt like I'd been punched by a professional boxer. Avery's smile faded. Bailey simply glanced down at her hands.

"All right. Because you asked me, I will not steal Christmas this year."

"Yes!" All the kids clapped again.

"But I make no promises for next year."

She wanted money for fucking Christmas dinner. Not only that, but she was in the damn hospital a week before, and for all I knew, she may not even make it home for the festivities.

One thing I knew for fucking sure was that I was going to pay for everything. I'd find out her name and be an angel donor.

Damn, that broke my heart.

"What do you all think about the pralines?" I asked. "Really good, right?"

The girl held up a small bag as if it was her most prized possession. "Bailey made my favorites with banana."

How did Bailey know her favorites?

I looked at my woman, who said, "Andrea has an autoimmune condition, and she makes a lot of trips here." She turned to face the kids. "I promise everyone will get their favorites delivered to their home next week."

Two of the kids jumped out of bed and went over to Bailey, hugging her.

I swallowed hard. The scene was impacting me in a way I couldn't explain. Damn, they all seemed attached to Bailey.

After each kid reiterated their favorites, making sure she knew them, we moved on to the next room. I carried the baskets that Avery and Bailey had brought with them.

"Thanks so much for being here and helping," Bailey said.

"I haven't helped at all yet."

"Oh, that joke with the Grinch was excellent," Avery exclaimed.

"Are those kids permanently in the hospital or something?"

"Oh no, nothing like that. Most of them are here for the first time."

"So, how can you possibly know their favorites, then?"

Bailey smiled sheepishly. For some reason, Avery was looking at me intently.

"We call up the morning before we come and ask the nurses if they can ask the kids what their favorite candies are, or what they usually like to eat. That gives us an idea. Then we make a lot of packages with everyone's favorites and mark them according to flavors. Then, when someone says they like cherry, we take the right package from the basket."

"They think we can do magic," Avery informed me.

For the next hour, we went from room to room, but we didn't have many left. The two of them had been here since midday, as I found out. In the last room, I didn't play the Grinch again but the Nutcracker. A girl said it was her favorite, and I immediately started doing a robotic walk—completely wrong interpretation, the girl assured me, but all the kids laughed anyway.

After we exited the final room, there were still some pralines left.

"I think we should leave these with the staff and call it an evening," Bailey said.

"Yep," Avery said. "I think so too."

"I'll take the baskets. I know where the head nurse is."

"I'll come with you," I offered.

"Not necessary. They're super easy to carry compared to when we arrived."

Bailey sauntered down the corridor while Avery and I waited by the elevator.

"It was nice of you showing up here," Avery said quietly.

"I wanted to catch up with Bailey."

"She lit up when you told her you were coming."

"I'm glad. You made a lot of kids happy."

"It's what we do."

"What are you not saying, Avery? You sound like you want to add something to that."

She sighed. "If you sell the confectionery, things like this would get lost."

I liked Avery. I appreciated her honesty and the way she faced everything.

"The charitable part could be easily done on the side," I countered, though I knew now that it wouldn't really be the same.

She pressed her lips together but didn't reply. I'd always considered the production side different from the charitable part, but for the first time, I was starting to have doubts. Bailey and Avery had called the hospital, asked about everyone's favorites, and then got to work. That simply wasn't something that happened in a for-profit company. Not ever.

I'd been to enough charity events to know how an evening like this would look. Someone would show up and deliver generic pralines. Or they'd employ clowns or other forms of entertainment, which wasn't bad per se. It was just that what Bailey and Avery did was different, deeper.

I was certain that those kids would remember this for quite some time. Bailey and Avery were involved in every aspect. Before tonight, I'd have seen that as a negative. But now I was starting to see the importance of such things. What these two had created was completely unique. There was a reason the LeBlanc & Broussard pralines were known throughout the whole city, and it wasn't just because of our name. It was because of the work they put in. Even though I was a numbers guy, I knew you couldn't possibly quantify this. But that didn't mean it was worthless. Quite the contrary—it was priceless.

Avery kept staring at me, arms folded over her chest as she leaned against the wall. She didn't say anything else, and Bailey joined us a few moments later. The basket she was holding was empty.

"All right, mission accomplished. Everyone's happy, kids and staff. We can go, and the weekend can start."

"I don't know how you still have so much energy left," Avery said. "My only plans for the weekend are to go home and sleep."

"I have enough energy for five people," Bailey said. "Doing things like this really pumps me up."

"What was your favorite moment of the evening?" I asked her.

"Probably when you started playing the Nutcracker."

"Yeah, I've got about a million pictures of that," Avery said. "It'll go in your hall of fame."

"Was I any good?" I asked. "I just did it based on what I remembered from seeing the movie, but it's been like a million years."

"No, you mostly did the robot dance, but it doesn't matter. It made the kids happy." Avery yawned, taking the empty baskets from Bailey. "I'm leaving. We only came with one car. Xander, I assume you're taking care of my sister tonight?"

I gave her a mock salute. "Yes, ma'am."

After Avery entered the elevator, Bailey looked at me.

"Aren't you meeting Bella?" she asked.

I pulled her to me, running my fingers through her hair. "I am, and I was actually going to ask you if you would like for us to spend the evening together, the three of us."

"I'd love that. Is your brother okay with it?"

"I'll text and ask, but I wouldn't think it would be a problem. I just wanted to clear it with you first."

"My talents with kids convinced you, huh?" she teased.

"That, and I want to spend the evening with you." I drew the tip of my nose from her temple down to her ear. There was no one else in the hallway; I assumed the visiting hours were over. "I thought about you a lot at the office."

"How come?"

I straightened up, tracing her jaw with my fingers. "Well, I was up in arms because everyone seemed to have taken off early. Then I imagined how much you'd make fun of me for thinking that."

Bailey burst out laughing, putting her arms around my neck. "Oh yes, I would. But you're forgiven because you played the role of the Grinch perfectly. I didn't even know you had it in you."

"Neither did I, but you're bringing out the playful side in me."

It was easy to let my guard down around Bailey. I wanted to impress her at every turn, and that was something totally new for me.

"Hey, would you wait here a second? I wanted to ask the nurses a couple of things." I wanted to make sure that little girl's bills were paid for, and I didn't want Bailey to know the details—just in case things didn't work out.

"Sure, I'll head to the main entrance."

A few minutes later, I caught back up with her as we headed out the door.

"What time do you have to be at your brother's house?" Bailey asked.

"About half an hour. If we hurry, we can even surprise Bella with beignets. Although, 'surprise' is probably the wrong choice of words. If I show my face there without them, I will never be invited again."

"Can you double-check with him if it's really okay that I come?" For some insane reason, she sounded apprehensive.

"My brother will have nothing against it," I assured her, but I texted him anyway.

Chad answered before we even got to the car, and I showed it to her.

Chad: Bella will probably be ecstatic that yet another uncle bit the dust.

"What's that supposed to mean?" Bailey inquired as we got in.

"Bella always complained that she wanted more women in the family. Both the grandmothers and my mom more than make up for it, but she's got a logic of her own."

"Kids usually do," she said in a soft voice.

"You really like kids, huh?" I asked as I sped toward Café du Monde.

"Yes. I hope to have three, maybe four."

"That's an overwhelming number," I said earnestly. I mean, I'd always assumed that I'd eventually have a family, but I never actively pursued it or thought about it too closely. But right now, I could see myself and Bailey surrounded by a few kids.

"You have five brothers."

"Hence why I know it's overwhelming. Though, I will say, the problem was that all of us were boys. It was a madhouse. Not sure how my parents and grandparents survived it. It took all six of them to keep up with all six of us, and we didn't even all come at once. Would you want boys and girls?"

I was genuinely interested in her answer.

"Hmm. A mix maybe. I'd definitely teach them how to make pralines, though, and I think girls would more likely love doing that."

"What exactly is it that you like about the process?"

"It's soothing. I mix ingredients and know something delicious will come out, and it'll make people happy. And me as well. Of course, kids have an interesting relationship with sweets. Best to operate with caution before introducing them to pralines too early. But I could imagine them sitting around me at the table at the confectionery. I'd give them small pieces of dough and let them play around with it."

"You're a very special soul, Bailey," I said quietly.

One I was quite attached to.

Chapter Twenty-Four

Xander

There was *a lot* happening at Café du Monde, but we got our beignets quickly enough.

"Oh, this is such an adorable home," Bailey said when we arrived at Chad's. "It's got so much character."

"It does," I said. "Also cracks and a very archaic ventilation and heating system and—"

"Hey, Mr. Grinch, you can get out of character now, okay?" She said this so seriously that I instantly burst out laughing.

The front door swung open. Chad nodded at me, then he turned to Bailey.

"Hi, Bailey, nice to see you again," he said.

"And you. Hi, Scarlett. Oh, your dress is amazing."

Scarlett instantly smiled, hoisting the baby up on her shoulder.

"You brought beignets too. Good instincts," Chad said. "Let us know if you need anything."

"We won't," I told him.

He always said that, but something truly major would have to happen for me to call him on a damn date.

"Bailey, thanks a lot for stopping by tonight," Scarlett said. "You had your hospital visit this evening, right?"

"Yes. It went really well. Xander here even successfully played the Grinch."

I'd never seen Chad shocked, but it was a sight to behold. He jerked his head back so fast, I was surprised he didn't get whiplash. His eyes were comically wide, his jaw hanging open. He closed it as if he'd just realized that.

"Wait, what? Was there a costume involved? Explain this. I need the details. Did you paint yourself green?"

"Don't be ridiculous," I replied.

"He didn't even need a costume. The kids bought his act even though he was wearing a suit and all. That's how convincing he was," Bailey said.

Scarlett only chuckled, but Chad burst out laughing. "One day we need the full details of the story," he said. "Preferably when the entire family is present."

I rolled my eyes. "You'll get it, I'm sure. Now go before you're too late and lose your reservation."

"Brother, it's only been a few minutes. No one boots you out of your place unless you're more than fifteen minutes late."

"You're already five minutes late," I pointed out.

"You with the details, always."

As they left, Bailey and I stepped inside.

"Bella?" I asked loudly.

"I'm in the kitchen, Uncle Xander."

When she was a little girl, she'd wait by the door and jump into my arms. I missed those days.

"Dad said you were coming with your girlf—" She stopped talking when she noticed Bailey. "Hi, Bailey."

I couldn't help but laugh. My niece had a penchant for calling everyone "girlfriend" when she saw them. Then again, it was true.

"It's nice to see you again, Bella."

"You brought beignets." She clapped her hands excitedly before grabbing the bag from Bailey.

"The girl knows what she wants," Bailey whispered as Bella brought the bag to the table.

"Yes, she does," I whispered back. "By the way, if she tries to talk us into watching *Goblet of Fire*, we have to say no."

"Chad doesn't allow it?" she asked.

"Exactly."

"I'll stand strong."

Bella started to grab plates for the table.

"We'll do that," I said.

"No, Uncle Xander. I'm a big girl now. I set the table all on my own every evening. I'm really good at it."

She set out three plates and then saw four beignets.

"Everyone gets one?" she asked.

"Exactly."

"So, what do we do with the fourth one?"

Bailey was looking at me intently.

"I can split it in three." I was only teasing her, but I could practically see the joy leave her eyes, and I couldn't do it for long. "Kidding, Bella. It's yours, of course."

"Yesssss. I haven't had beignets since we went to Café du Monde."

"I find that hard to believe."

"Fine," Bella said. "Dad sometimes buys them for me, but I'm only allowed one."

I didn't blame him, but it was Friday, so she didn't have to get up early for school tomorrow. Besides, as everyone liked to remind me, we had one week to go before Christmas. Rules could be broken.

"What do you want us to do tonight, Bella?" Bailey asked as we ate our beignets.

Bella sucked in her breath, looking straight at Bailey. "We could watch *Goblet of Fire.*"

Damn, I was good. I'd been about to wait to warn Bailey until after we ate, but my instincts were on point, as usual.

Bailey had an excellent poker face, though. She didn't seem either surprised or amused, though I knew her well enough to tell that she was both.

"I remember that being a very dark movie, Bella. Does your dad allow you to watch it?"

The thing about Bella was that she never lied. Sure, she tried to negotiate, but she didn't lie.

"No." Her shoulders slumped. "But if I watch it with an adult and you think it's okay, then maybe he won't mind."

She might not lie, but she did like to sneak around.

"We can't do that. We don't want your dad to stop trusting us. Then he would never let us come around again, and how would you get your two beignets?"

Bella frowned, starting to eat her second one. She had powdered sugar in her hair. She'd done that ever since she was a baby. In the beginning, I used to clean it up after every bite, but eventually I realized it was easier to just let her finish eating before cleaning her up. Of course, that had been years ago. These days, she went to check her appearance in the bathroom mirror and took care of the powdered sugar all on her own.

"But I have a suggestion," Bailey said. "I mean, you can totally say no."

Bella perked up. "Yes?"

"What if we rewatch your favorite Harry Potter movie and discuss it?"

Bella looked at me skeptically. "Uncle Xander, have you seen any yet?"

"The first one. We watched together, don't you remember?"

She groaned. "That was two years ago. Hmm. Then we have to watch the second one or Uncle Xander won't understand any of it."

I wanted to point out that I'd totally erased it from my mind, so I didn't remember the first one either, but that seemed like the wrong thing to say. "I'm open to anything."

"*Chamber of Secrets* is the one with the basilisk, right?" Bailey asked.

Bella looked at her as if she'd hung the moon. How could she relate to kids so easily, even those at the hospital? She'd been able to form a connection with every single one of them even though she'd only met some of them that very evening.

"Exactly. It is a bit scary," Bella admitted. "When I read the book, I didn't imagine the basilisk to be so frightening. It looked more like a snake to me, not a dragon."

"I thought the same thing. I don't know why, though. It did say it had scales. But maybe I imagined a snake because it was far less scary."

"You got scared too?" Bella asked, mouth hanging open.

"Oh yeah. And in the beginning, when Harry was hearing all those whispers from the wall and we didn't know what it was, that was even scarier."

I didn't think Bailey was making it all up. But she was clearly adding some dramatic effects for Bella.

"Yes, exactly. Me too. I was reading it under my covers with a flashlight because Dad said I was only allowed to read a few pages a day." As I said, the girl was sneaky! "But once you start reading Harry Potter, you can't just read a few pages. I'm not sure why he thinks that."

"I'll have to take your side on that."

Bella looked like she wanted to jump over the table and hug Bailey. Instead, she simply ate her beignet at a faster pace. Harry Potter was always a fantastic motivator for her.

Since Bailey and I only had one, we finished first. Then Bailey looked around.

"You already have a Christmas tree," she remarked.

"Yes," Bella said breathlessly, mouth full of beignet. "It's all in Gryffindor colors."

"Red and gold. It's truly beautiful!"

"Thank you. We love it too. Okay, I'm done. I'll clean myself up, and then we can start watching. Uncle Xander, could you turn on the TV?"

I nodded. "Sure."

Once Bella was out of earshot, I told Bailey, "You opened a can of worms, just so you know."

We both rose from the table. I intended to go to the living room but then got another idea. I pushed her against the edge of the table and feathered my mouth over hers.

"Xander!"

"This is going to be the last chance I get to kiss you like this tonight. Bella will hold us hostage here until the movie ends. And I've been wanting to kiss you ever since we were at the hospital."

"By all means, then, get your fill," she teased.

I captured her mouth the next second. I knew I would never have enough of Bailey, just as I knew that my name was Xander LeBlanc. She tasted like powdered sugar. I deepened the kiss, holding her waist. She felt so damn good against my body. I sucked on her tongue and practically felt the second she started to get turned on. She pressed her thighs together and pushed her chest into me. I only pulled back because I heard footsteps, stepping away just in time.

"Uncle Xander, did you start the movie?" Bella asked impatiently.

I cleared my throat. "No, not yet."

"Why? What were you doing?"

"We were..."

"Kissing?" she asked.

I nearly swallowed my tongue. Bailey gasped. "No, we were preparing to clean the table." She turned around quickly, grabbing the plates.

"I know about things like that. Sometimes I spy on Dad and Scarlett when they kiss. I don't know why they're trying to hide. I like that they love each other. It makes me happy."

Her explanation completely put me at ease. I wasn't touching Bailey inappropriately, or doing anything more than kissing. Granted, I would've preferred Bella not to see us at all, but it never occurred to me that seeing adults show affection could make a kid feel happy and safe. I tried to think back to my own childhood and realized Mom and Dad were always like that with each other—a quick peck on the lips or a hug were daily occurrences. We'd grown up like that.

After depositing everything in the dishwasher, we went to the living room. "Do you know if Netflix or Prime has the Potter series?" Bailey asked.

"Dad bought the movies for me on Prime, so I have all of them even though I'm not allowed to watch them."

If I wasn't careful, she was going to start her propaganda again for *Goblet of Fire*. "*Chamber of Secrets* it is." I immediately started the movie, and Bella hopped into her favorite armchair next to the couch. Bailey and I were sitting next to each other. I put an arm around her waist, pulling her as close as possible to me.

"Don't you dare fondle me," she whispered in my ear.

"I wouldn't dream of it," I whispered back. Only now that she'd put the idea in my mind, all I could think about was ways to do that without Bella catching on. I was like a teenager, figuring out ways to grope the girl I liked, which was completely unlike me. I couldn't even remember the last time I'd felt like that. But then again, being around Bailey brought out this side of me, and I wasn't sorry about it. Not in the slightest.

I'd spent the past few years focusing on numbers and numbers alone. Sure, it had paid off—the Orleans Conglomerate was far more profitable than it had been before I dug into the books—but I'd let a lot of things slide in the process.

Some of my brothers, like Julian and Zachary, not to mention the younger ones, had found a balance. Their businesses did fantastic, and they also had fun. But I'd denied myself that for too long. No more.

As the credits popped up on the screen, I scrolled through my emails. Ron Trudeau sent me one about the confectionery, but I didn't want to open it right now. I made a mental note to reply first thing Monday morning.

"See, I'm already starting to get mad at the Dursleys," Bailey said when the first scene came on, and I realized on the spot that she knew her Potter stuff and hadn't been faking the interest earlier for Bella's benefit.

"They're such mean people."

She totally enjoyed chatting with Bella, and I was so caught up in the passionate way she defended Harry that I wasn't even paying attention to the movie. I just wanted to watch Bailey.

Chapter Twenty-Five
Xander

It was past midnight when we left Chad and Scarlett's house.

"I loved this," Bailey exclaimed. "Just putting it out there, but whenever Bella gets the green light that she can watch the next Harry Potter movie, I volunteer to watch it with her."

I pulled her close to me, laughing. "You really mean that, don't you?"

She nodded. "Oh yeah." Then her eyes widened. "I mean, I wasn't implying that... Oh, shoot."

"What is it?"

"Well, that could take a while."

"Probably. Knowing Chad, he's going to make her wait another year or two."

Bailey was still looking away, and then it dawned on me. She didn't know what was going to happen in a year or two. Frankly, neither did I, but the thought of coming here with her to watch the next installment of that godforsaken movie franchise sounded good. I could do anything with her and would be totally fine with it.

"It would be my pleasure to watch the next one with you. If anything, you'll make it more enjoyable."

She looked up at me with a smile as we started to walk again.

I held her hand, interlacing our fingers. Neither of us was wearing gloves, and the temperature had dropped. But that wasn't the only reason why I was holding her hand. I liked this contact.

"So, that thought doesn't scare you?" she asked.

"What?" I was doing this on purpose because I wanted to hear her thoughts first.

"Oh, why are you like that?"

"Because I want to know what's going on in that pretty mind of yours."

"I'm not even sure. I like planning ahead and thinking about the future, but..."

"This seems fast," I finished for her.

She nodded, her smile dropping a bit.

"It is fast, but you know what? It feels damn right." I wrapped an arm around her waist. Clearly just touching her fingers wasn't enough.

"I know. I usually go with the flow," she whispered, "but not you, Mr. LeBlanc."

"Not me. You've got that right," I admitted. "But this is different." I felt it in my bones. I'd never felt as close to anyone as I did with Bailey.

I kissed the corner of her mouth, and she sighed. "You're going to make me swoon in the street, aren't you?"

I was about to answer when her stomach rumbled.

I laughed. "First I'm going to feed you."

"Mm. What are we having? I was starting to get a bit hungry at the house, but I was ashamed to say anything."

"They always have excellent food. Next time, just look in the fridge."

She blinked rapidly at the words "next time."

"Scarlet cooks in her free time?"

"Not as much, but Chad does, and he's skilled in the kitchen."

I looked at her intently. She still seemed to be processing the "next time" thing. I was confident about it. I wanted Bailey to be part of my life more than I wanted anything else.

"Where exactly are we going?" she asked.

"How do you feel about po' boys?"

Her eyes widened. "Helloooo? I love them."

I chuckled. "Had to ask. After all, you said you're not a beignet girl."

"I know, but still. I was born and bred in NOLA. I do like most of our treats. I just think beignets are overrated."

"Don't let Bella hear you say that. She won't be a fan of you any longer."

"My lips are sealed." She mimed the action, laughing. "So, where is it exactly?"

"Just around the corner. I often grab one if I'm in the area. It's my favorite po' boy."

"Must be a fancy place."

I wondered why she'd say that. "It's actually not. It's just a take-out spot."

"You're joking."

I frowned. "No. Why?"

"I thought you always had fancy meals in one form or another."

As we turned to the left, I pointed in front of us. "Here it is."

Her eyes lit up. "A mom-and-pop shop. I love those!"

The shop was empty at this hour. We both ordered chicken po' boys with all the toppings they offered and then stepped out on the street with our sandwiches. Bailey bit into hers right away.

"Ohhhhh, I'll remember this place. Truly one of the best I've had."

"Whenever you're in the mood for it, just tell me and I'll bring it to you."

"In-person delivery?" She batted her eyelashes.

I nodded. "Of course. Only the best for you."

"I wasn't expecting you to agree so fast. Can we make it a naked delivery?" She wiggled her eyebrows.

I growled. "Woman!"

"Okay. Okay, let's eat." She started to shiver as she took another bite.

"Want to hurry to the car?"

"Sure. Or you can keep me warm."

"We can do both." I was going to, anyway.

I put my free arm on her back, moving it up and down. It didn't take us long to finish the po' boys. Just as we were done eating, we passed a group of carolers who were singing in front of a mansion along the way.

"I used to do that with Avery a lot as a kid."

"Why am I not surprised?" I teased. And then I couldn't help myself. I lowered my mouth toward her ear and tugged at her earlobe.

"Xander...," she chastised, and I straightened up. Clearing her throat, she added, "It was a nice tradition. Didn't you go with your brothers?"

"Actually, I did."

"Ha. I knew it. No one can live in New Orleans and not go caroling."

"I'm pretty sure there are some people who don't, but that wasn't how we did things in my family."

"Then you have to know some carols."

"Of course I do. Vaguely. Like I said, I go caroling in Jackson Square with the family every year."

"Right, I remember you told me that. Avery and I do that too. I, for one, can't wait to have kids. Then I'll have a perfectly good excuse to go with them. They'll need a chaperone, obviously."

I stopped walking, just watching Bailey as she watched the group. "I'd give you some of that eggnog to take caroling with you."

Bailey immediately looked at me, her breath catching. She cleared her throat. "Alcoholic or nonalcoholic?"

"Everyone would have separate flasks," I said, a picture of the future filling my mind. "You would have one with alcohol, and the kids would have their own—without alcohol, of course."

"And you?" Bailey whispered.

"I would be the chauffeur who picks you up, since you'll be tipsy." I'd never had any train of thought that led me this way before, at least not one that was so vivid and full of details.

Bailey would be dressed just as now, maybe with a cap on her head. We'd have possibly three kids. They'd know all the carols by heart.

"What would it take to hypothetically convince you to go caroling with us?" she asked.

"That would not happen," I countered.

"Why not? I could even share my eggnog with you."

I threw my head back, laughing. "You're trying to bribe me using my own eggnog?"

"I mean, the problem would be that we'd then need a designated driver," she pondered.

"We could just Uber, or I'm sure one of my brothers wouldn't mind chaperoning us. Here's a thought, actually." The ideas were free-flowing now—which also never happened to me. I never dealt in what-ifs or imagined futures. I was a facts man. But this was fun. "We could go in a bigger group."

"Does Bella go caroling?"

"Yeah, she does. Anthony and Beckett go with her, sometimes Zachary too."

"I see. So, they're easily corrupted when it comes to caroling."

I nodded, moving closer to her once more. "Yes. But I'm easily corruptible too. For certain things."

"Not caroling."

I shook my head. "Absolutely not."

"Oh, you're such a Grinch."

"Stop saying that or I'll kiss you right here in the middle of the street," I growled.

"And you think I don't want that? What gave you that idea?"

I pressed my lips to hers the next second. Though I couldn't kiss her the way I wanted to because we'd make a spectacle of ourselves, and there were kids around.

When I straightened up, I noticed two of the kids watching us.

"Don't want to be a bad influence on those kids," I said, nodding to them.

Bailey turned to watch and giggled. "Whoops, we're drawing attention to ourselves. So, you'd like to be a role model, huh, Mr. Grinch?"

"You call me that one more time..."

"And? What do I get?" She batted her eyelashes. "You'll throw me over your shoulder and take me to the penthouse?"

"I so fucking will."

She bit her lower lip.

"Why don't we move toward the car?"

"Good idea." Her voice was uneven.

I was going to spend the night pleasuring this woman. I was already making plans.

Fuck, I needed to change the topic right now or else we'd never make it to the penthouse.

"So, what other Christmas traditions does your family have?" I was genuinely curious about it.

"Mom and Dad weren't big on celebrating growing up."

I couldn't let this opportunity pass. "And how do you feel about that?"

She elbowed me lightly. "I think it's a missed opportunity. Christmas should always be celebrated, no matter if there are kids in the house or not."

"My grandparents and parents agree with you."

"You act like you're completely different, yet you have your traditions with Bella."

"I do a lot of things for Bella," I admitted. "I like making her happy." As we reached the car, I added, "Sometimes I think I should make more of an effort." I opened the door for her. "This year it's become even clearer."

She leaned against the seat, looking up at me. "How come?"

"I thought that honoring my family's legacy meant making sure the company was doing better than ever. Always improving profit margins, processes, and so on. It was my top goal. And it still is. It probably always will be. But I realized that I've been spending less time with my family over the years, and it's a pity. I mean, Bella will soon be all grown up."

"I think you've still got a few years."

"My grandparents and parents won't be around forever, yet I've spent the past few Christmases cooped up in my office."

"There's always time to change that. I can't believe the Christmas spirit is rubbing off on you." Her smile was delightful.

"It's not that," I assured her, resting my fingertips on her neck. "You're making me see things in a different light."

"Really? How come?"

"I can't explain it. Your way of looking at things. The fact that you were willing to completely change careers because you were no longer happy doing what you were doing. That's admirable. And now you're doing something that makes you completely happy. You make me question myself in all the good ways."

"And I have a few more ideas concerning you."

"I can't wait for you to share them with me in front of that fireplace you like so much."

She grinned. "Hell yes."

CHAPTER TWENTY-SIX
BAILEY

On the twenty-fourth of December, I was ready to call it a year. I'd done all the deliveries, but I still headed to the confectionery. It was my tradition to come here on Christmas Eve. No one else was working, and I enjoyed having the place to myself. I made a pot of mulled wine and played carols while I made the last batch of pralines for the year. I was taking them to the bonfire celebration in Algiers this afternoon, right before heading to Jackson Square for caroling.

I'd put the pralines in the oven and was starting to clean up the counter. Since I wasn't expecting anyone at all, I startled when I heard someone call out from the yard.

"Hello? Is this the LeBlanc-Broussard confectionery?"

I took off my apron and hurried outside. A young guy, maybe a few years older than me, was waiting there, looking around with curiosity.

"Yes, this is us. Well, it's just me today," I said. "My name is Bailey. What can I do for you?"

"I'm Ron Trudeau. Not sure if anyone from the Orleans Conglomerates told you, but I'm interested in buying the confectionery."

Every muscle in my body stiffened. I swear to God, I forgot how to breathe for a few seconds.

Xander found a buyer. Why didn't he tell me?

I drew in a deep breath and blinked a few times because my vision was unfocused. Then I clasped my hands in front of me and nodded. "No one told me you were coming."

"I did tell Xander. I mean, he's the only one I spoke to."

Oh, man, this is just getting worse. I put a hand on my chest and shook my head. *It doesn't matter. Surely there's some explanation for his not mentioning a potential buyer.* Though I couldn't help but feel slighted by the whole thing. As close as we'd become and then this? It hurt.

"What can I do for you?" I asked.

"Before I make an actual offer, I want to take a look around. Would you mind showing me? I totally understand if you can't. I mean, it's Christmastime, and you're probably very busy. But I thought I'd drop by on the off chance anyway."

I carefully considered my next steps. I couldn't possibly kick him out.

You don't own this place, Bailey. You're an employee of the Orleans Conglomerate, and you knew, deep down, this day would come.

So, even though it was killing my heart, I smiled and said, "Sure, come on in. Everyone else is on vacation already."

"If you're busy, I can look around by myself."

"Nah, you're going to understand this place better if I walk you through it. Let's start with the kitchen."

He followed me inside, looking around at everything. "Oh, you're listening to Christmas music! How fitting."

"Yeah. Let me just turn down the volume." Grabbing my phone, I minimized the sound. "Now, about the kitchen. The ovens were all replaced a few years ago, and they're in perfect condition."

"They look good. I've loved these pralines since I was a kid. I was so surprised when word got out that the LeBlancs are looking to sell it."

I just smiled at him. What could I do?

"Are you in the same industry?" I asked.

"We do sweets."

"More than just pralines?"

"I mean, we do pralines, too, but they don't taste nearly as good as yours. Did you develop the recipes?"

"We took some over, but my sister and I keep coming up with new ones."

"I snapped up some pralines at the light festival. They were amazing as usual."

"Thank you." I pointed to the door closest to us. "So, that's the supply room. The boxes are delivered to us, as well as the individual plastic wraps."

He frowned. "So, who puts them together?"

"We do."

"How many employees are there?"

"There are four of us. Only my sister and I bake, but we're also jacks-of-all-trades, doing deliveries, packaging, and everything else."

He frowned slightly. "It's not how I would do things, but if it's working for you, that's good. Can you show me the rest of the building? I just want to see all the assets and think about what they'd be worth. I still haven't had an asking price from Xander, and I want to know what to expect."

Assets. That sounded so cold and soulless, but he was right. That's what this was.

"There's not much more to see, just another storage room." I opened the door. There was no window in here.

He poked his head inside. "I could add another wing, more ovens."

"So, you expect to expand the operation, then?" I swallowed hard.

"Yes. I'd love to bring my own team, of course. I did tell Xander that I would very much like to convince you to hand over your recipes."

Another shock went through me. *Hand over?* I didn't have a stack of recipes. They were all in my mind.

"What's your feeling about that?"

"I'll have to think about it," I said noncommittally.

"Yes, of course. But, I mean, they're not your intellectual property. The recipes belong to the Orleans Conglomerate."

I hated business talk. I really did. "I know that. But all of this requires a lot of consideration."

He nodded once. "True."

"Could I ask when you would plan to go through with this?"

"Not until next year, if at all."

I was starting to feel a bit hopeful even though I still felt utterly betrayed. Why would Xander not even give me a heads-up? I'd told him I didn't want us to talk about business, but being blindsided by this guy was... Well, I didn't like it at all.

"These things take time," he continued. "It wouldn't be as much work as an actual takeover would be because this isn't big enough to do the usual evaluation. But it would probably take until well after Mardi Gras to finish everything."

"Right. Mm-hmm. So, you would be keeping the recipes?" I asked him.

"Yes, of course. That's the reason I'm buying it. I'm still working with Xander to allow me to use the LeBlanc & Broussard logo, but that's going to be a tough negotiation."

I raised a brow. "How so?"

"He insists that he doesn't want the family name on anything that isn't part of the Orleans Conglomerate anymore, but we'll see. It's still early days, and I've got a lot of things working in my favor, such as the fact that this place doesn't actually make money. It's just bleeding on his books, which is why he wants to get rid of it."

Oh, my poor heart. I couldn't take this anymore. Since I'd shown him around the few rooms we had, we went back outside and circled the building once.

"No warehouse?" he asked.

"It's not really necessary. We don't buy anything in bulk. Things could happen if we did, like the flour going bad from humidity and so on. We've had a lot of things happen over the years, so now we buy everything as fresh as possible. The storage room is more than enough. Besides, it's only ever really full during the Christmas season." I swallowed hard as we walked toward the front gate. "A lot of our work is for charity. Would you continue with that?"

I was afraid to even ask, but I had to know. Though, if he said no, what could I do? Nothing. Absolutely nothing. I hated being so powerless.

"Of course. That's the best marketing I can get."

My heart moved back into its right place.

"But if you can't use the LeBlanc & Broussard logo, then what's the point?"

He tilted his head. "That will make things a bit more complicated, but if we keep showing up at the same events where you've been for years, that would help spread the word that it's the same product. But we would have to come up with another marketing plan regardless."

I wasn't entirely convinced, and I could tell he wasn't either, but I didn't press the issue.

He smiled. "Thanks a lot for indulging me, and on Christmas Eve no less. I assume Xander will be in touch about whatever will happen next."

"I'm sure he will." *Or not, considering he didn't even tell me about you showing up.*

"I wish you a great Christmas, Bailey."

"And you too."

I meant it, despite everything. Everyone deserved to have a nice, relaxed holiday.

After he left, I headed back to the kitchen. Grabbing my phone, I turned the volume back up on my carols, needing to get into the Christmas spirit now more than ever. I also needed to keep my pralines from burning, so I rounded the counter and checked the oven—albeit with a heavy heart.

Xander

"All right, let's call it a day," I told Lydia when she came into my office after lunch with a huge stack of documents.

She smiled. "I was just going to ask if I could leave two hours early."

"You can take off now."

"And you?"

"I'll be going too."

Her jaw dropped for a second before she caught herself. "Progress. Merry Christmas, Xander."

"Merry Christmas."

I glanced at the documents on the desk. They could wait until after the holidays.

I was about to get up from my chair when I got a call from Ron Trudeau. *Shit!* I'd completely forgotten to open his email, and then it got buried by others on Monday morning. I answered right away, not wanting him to think I wasn't serious.

"Hi, Xander."

"Hi, Ron"

"I figured I'd call you since the last email—"

"I want to apologize for that. I completely overlooked it."

"That would explain a few things."

I frowned, jumping up from my desk. "What things?"

"I went by the confectionery, and Bailey gave me a tour. But she was very surprised to see me there."

Fuck, fuck, fuck. "You were at the confectionery?" I said, as if he hadn't made it abundantly clear.

"Yes."

"When?"

"Just now. I'm on my way out." *Fuck. Bailey must think I'm the biggest asshole in the world.* "So anyway, the place looks solid. I'd make some changes, but the bare bones are there. I asked her about the recipes, but she wasn't very straightforward."

"That wasn't your request to make," I barked.

"I figured you might react like that. Definitely wasn't smart to bring that up. I don't think she liked it either."

No shit. Jesus Christ, what must Bailey be thinking right now?

"Listen, I don't want to cut you short. I was actually going to ask you to lunch before Christmas, but one thing happened and then another, and... I've decided not to sell."

Ron groaned. "LeBlanc, come on. You were set on that. We haven't even talked price yet."

"It's not about the price, I just have other plans for it."

"Well, this was a waste of time." He sounded very annoyed, and I couldn't blame him, as this wasn't my most professional moment.

"I apologize. How can I make it up to you?"

"I don't know that you can. You're known around business circles as a man of your word. I didn't think you'd put out feelers for selling something if you didn't actually have the intention to do so."

"I had every intention back then, but things have changed in the meantime."

"What changed? Did the business suddenly turn a profit?"

"No, it didn't. Far from it." But I'd since learned that that wasn't the most important thing. That the LeBlanc & Broussard pralines meant something entirely different to those who got them. And I owed that all to Bailey. I needed to talk to her. "Listen, I'll set up a meeting in the new year, okay?"

He scoffed. "Don't bother. Just be straightforward from now on."

I disliked that he was questioning my reputation, but I had more important things to focus on, like Bailey.

"Listen, I have to go right now."

"I've got better things to do, too, than continue wasting my time. Merry fucking Christmas."

Well, that was an attitude, but if I were in his shoes, I'd be pissed off too.

The second he hung up, I called Bailey. *Please pick up, Bailey. Pick up, pick up.*

She didn't, though. I didn't blame her. Was she still at the confectionery, or had she headed home? I decided to go to the confectionery first. I should be there in about forty minutes.

Of course, I forgot that it being Christmas Eve. The entire city was absolute madness. Getting out of the business district alone took me just under an hour. I ran into congested streets at every turn. Throughout the drive, I kept calling Bailey, but she didn't pick up. After five tries, I gave up. I wrote three long texts while I waited at red lights, then deleted all of them. Any explanation sounded completely stupid in writing. I needed to talk to her in person.

An hour and a half later, I finally made it to the confectionery. It was closed. The front door had five locks on it, which meant Bailey had gone home. I cursed, pushing at the gate for no reason before turning around and going back to the car.

I called Bailey again, to no avail. I could go straight to her house, but what if she wasn't there?

Then I got another idea. I got in the car and called Avery's number. To my intense relief, she answered.

"Hi, Avery, this is—"

"Xander, I know."

"You sound upset."

"Yeah, you could say that."

"Bailey told you about Trudeau's visit?"

"Yes, and I can't believe you. How could you let her be blindsided like that? She trusted you."

"Avery, I'm going to need to get a word in."

She huffed into the phone. "Fine. What do you have to say for yourself?"

"I didn't know the guy was coming."

"He said he emailed you."

I sighed. "I was with your sister when he emailed over the weekend, and I forgot to even look at it."

"So, you didn't know he was going to show up?" Her tone had softened a little.

"No."

I heard her take a deep breath, then release it slowly, as though she was calming herself down. "Okay, now I'm ready to give you the benefit of the doubt."

"I want to talk to Bailey."

"You have to get past me first." I'd laugh, but this was typical sibling behavior. If anyone tried to put one over on any of my brothers, parents, or grandparents, I'd be even worse than Avery right now. "Why didn't you tell her you were so close to selling? She's so heartbroken."

"Fuck. That was the last thing I wanted. Listen, long story short is that this guy contacted me a while ago. I've changed my views on many things in the meantime."

"Such as?"

"This is something I'd like to discuss with Bailey directly. Do you know where she is?"

Avery hesitated for a split second, then said, "Yeah, she's with me."

Of course. "May I speak with her?"

"And she's upset."

"I could be at your house—"

She laughed. "In a million years. Trust me, the traffic is an absolute nightmare."

"It's going to be like that around the whole city anyway. I want to see your sister today."

"She'll be in the city a bit later."

"When?"

"Why? What do you have in mind?"

"That's not something I'm going to discuss with you."

She laughed. "Oh, good. It means you're going to put in an effort. She completely deserves that."

"She deserves the very fucking best in this world."

"You mean that, Xander?"

"Yes. And maybe this is too much information, but I want her to know that the time I've spent with her was too amazing to ruin it with any business talk."

"Sounds like you appreciate my sister. You get a lot of points for that."

"Where exactly is she going to be today?"

"Well, obviously we're going to be caroling at Jackson Square."

"So will my family, but I need to see her before that," I replied on a groan.

"She'll be at a bonfire celebration before. I don't know where, though. Don't hijack her time there. She takes all these Christmas events very seriously."

"I know. Avery, don't worry. I just want her to know how much I care about her." I couldn't find the right way to explain, but it didn't matter. Bailey was the one who needed to hear it, not Avery.

"She's taking a nap right now. She was a bit spent." Jesus Christ, she'd been so worn out that she needed to nap? That was so unlike Bailey. "But as soon as she wakes up, I'll ask her which bonfire she's going to."

"All right." I checked the clock. I was going to look at all the places with bonfires. "Does she usually go out of the city a lot? As far as I know, none of them are in New Orleans."

"No. My money is on Algiers Point. She's gone there often over the years. That way, she can come back to the square for caroling without having to hurry. But I don't know for sure."

"Then please find out," I replied.

By the time we hung up, my mind was already spinning, considering all the logistics. I'd make it work no matter where she went for that bonfire.

I'd go to the fucking moon for Bailey.

Chapter Twenty-Seven
Bailey

I loved the bonfire tradition. The one in Algiers Point was my favorite because I could make back to the French Quarter in time for the Christmas caroling event after, and that was something I never wanted to miss.

I kept the bag of pralines close to my chest as I stepped off the ferry. It was very crowded, and I was afraid someone would bump into me and knock everything from my hands.

Even though my heart was heavy, I was determined to enjoy this evening and focus on all the good things I had going on. My life was amazing. I was completely healthy, and so was my family. Avery and I had a strong bond, and our online business was thriving. Since the confectionery was going to close down, we'd had to double our efforts on it. The videos we already had made and listed in the course library were generating good money, but if it became our sole source of income, we'd have to upload new content much more often.

Xander had called a few times, but I didn't pick up. I honestly didn't know what to say to him. I was still shocked that he'd found a buyer and didn't even give me a heads-up.

He'd always said that he'd decide after Christmas. I took that to mean that he'd only start searching for a seller in January. Maybe that was my fault, and I should've asked him to be more specific.

Then again, I knew Xander's business motto. He got things done, and thoughts and feelings had no bearing. Ruthless for a good cause... right? The confectionery wasn't making a profit, so why not sell it? *Sigh.*

But right now, I truly didn't want to think about it anymore. Instead, I focused on the structure of the bonfire and smiled, heading that way.

The structure hanging over the fire changed every year. This year, there were circles floating over the mass of wood that they'd light up. Sometimes I could easily tell what it was and sometimes I couldn't at all. But I enjoyed it nonetheless.

The market was already bustling with life. There were a lot of food options. Most were traditional offerings like gumbo or jambalaya, but there were plenty who had burgers and fries. Someone was making beignets too; I could smell them no matter where I was, but I couldn't see them yet. My favorite section was the one where art vendors displayed their work. I wanted to check it out, but first I needed to drop off some of the pralines.

I went over to Andrea Scott. She was serving baked potatoes with all sorts of toppings as usual. My favorite combo was cheese, bacon, and cranberry. It sounded weird, but it was delicious.

"Hey," she greeted, me, "you brought pralines."

"Of course. I couldn't come to the bonfire without them."

"You're such a doll."

Her whole family was working the cart. She had twelve-year-old twin boys milling around. Her husband, John, was currently chopping at mad speed, and I didn't want to interrupt him.

There was a line, too, so I just told her, "I'll be around here later."

"Of course."

I went by the art section right away, moving faster now that my basket was half empty. I knew the paintings were farther down the line, but I took my time glancing at all sorts of trinkets and handmade Christmas decorations. They were lovely.

Everyone had decorated their tables with twinkle lights and small Santa Claus figurines. I could feel my entire body relaxing as I spent more time here. I guess I shouldn't be so upset, as I had a lot to be thankful for. And I reminded myself again that our online business was a great plan for our future. But it was still difficult not to feel disappointed.

"You're a tough customer," Xander's voice said as I moved on to another cart without purchasing anything.

I jumped, turning around. "What are you doing here?" My heart rate accelerated so fast that my ears buzzed for a few seconds. I took in deep breaths to calm myself down.

"I spoke to Avery," he said softly. "She told me you would be here."

"When did you arrive?"

"The ferry before you. I waited to catch you in a good moment. We need to talk."

I looked down at my feet. "Sure. I'm sorry I didn't take your calls."

"You don't have to apologize. If I were you, I wouldn't have taken them either."

I looked back up at him. My heart was thundering.

"Want us to move a bit to the side?" he asked, and I nodded. I didn't want to be in anyone's way. And I also didn't want the vendor overhearing our conversation.

"Sure, let's go over there." I pointed to a darker space where there were no tables set up and we wouldn't be bothering anyone.

I shivered as we stepped into the darkness. Xander didn't miss it. "Are you cold? I can give you my coat."

"No, I'm just... well, I'm stressed out."

He frowned. "Bailey, please don't be."

"Xander, I really don't want to fight on Christmas Eve, but why didn't you tell me anything?"

He looked straight at me. "First of all, I didn't know he was going to stop by the confectionery today."

"Ron said he informed you."

"I saw his email when we were watching Harry Potter with Bella, but I didn't open it. I figured I'd deal with it on Monday, and then I completely forgot about it."

This was already making things just a bit better, but still. "When did you start talking to him?" I asked, fiddling with my fingers behind my back.

"When I decided that I wanted to revamp the confectionery business, I put out feelers. I went to a business lunch with a few people in the industry and told them about my plan. I encouraged them to spread the word and tell anyone who was interested to get in touch with my company."

"But that means you never gave the confectionery a chance." I was getting upset now. "I thought you weren't going to decide until after Christmas?"

"And I was, but putting out feelers means I'd know if there was any interest at all. It's efficient," he explained, and I actually started to laugh.

"Of course! I forgot."

"I wasn't going to make any definitive move before Christmas, though, no matter what."

"Oh, Xander. Why didn't you tell me there was even any interest? I know I always shut down business talk, but this is major."

Xander tilted closer, touching my cheek. "I never wanted to spoil our moments together by bringing this up. I knew it would sour the mood. I was too hungry for every moment I could spend with you to ruin it. I was completely selfish, and I'm sorry."

"Then please be honest with me right now. When is it going to happen?"

"What?"

"The sale."

He shook his head. "It's not going to happen."

"What?" My heart was now truly out of control. Not only because he was touching me, but also because I was starting to feel hopeful for the first time since this morning.

"We're not going to sell the confectionery."

"Are you serious? But why? What made you change your mind?"

"Well, I will be making some changes. But we can discuss them with Avery in the new year. I want to grow the business, but in a way that stays personal. You convinced me, Bailey, showing me all the passion you put into it."

Warmth invaded my heart all of a sudden. I put a hand on my chest. "Xander, are you serious?"

"Yes. Why is that so hard to believe?"

"Because you're so stubborn. I didn't think you'd change your mind."

"I don't think anyone ever changed my mind until you." I smiled at him, and though I tried to make it small and delicate, of course I couldn't. I could feel it taking over my entire face.

"You've shown me how important other things are besides efficiency and numbers."

"Now you're trying to talk your way into my pants," I teased.

"Of course I am, but I also mean every word. Bailey, you've enriched my life in ways I can't even put into words. You mean everything to me. Please believe that I'd never blindside you with something like that. I love you far too much to hurt you."

I closed my eyes, putting my hands on my chest. "I want to take a moment to savor these words and keep them right here."

"Fuck, I love you more with every passing second, I swear."

"Not more than I love you, Xander. Today, after that guy left, I realized that I was mad, but I also loved you far too much. So that's why I didn't answer the phone. I wasn't sure what to do. I didn't want to fight."

"Because it's Christmas."

I opened one eye. "And because I love you."

He grinned. "Glad we got that settled."

Xander glanced around. "You know, I've never been to a bonfire celebration."

I just gasped, unable to comprehend how he'd never been to one after living in the city his whole life.

"It's festive," he said. "Will we catch the actual bonfire being lit up?"

I hesitated. "Well, not really. That's the part I usually miss because the caroling starts roughly around that time."

"Then what do you usually do when you're here?"

"I just soak it all up." I clapped my hands excitedly.

"Then I'll soak it up with you. Actually, I'm just going to enjoy you."

"You sweet talker."

"I try my best."

He draped his whole body around mine somehow, keeping an arm around my shoulder but also walking slightly behind me. I realized he was trying to shield me from the cold. Oh yeah, a true Southern gentleman.

A band had started to play carols. I looked up at him with a grin. "Carols are allowed on Christmas Eve, right? Even for the Grinch?"

"Bailey," he growled in my ear.

"Well, I have to be certain."

"You did get me quite used to the carols."

"Really? So you listen to them at the office?" I asked as we ventured toward stands with more trinkets.

"Let's not get ahead of ourselves."

"My bad. Oh, the air smells like sweetcorn," I said, catching a whiff on the wind.

"Think you know who's boiling it?"

"I'm pretty sure. Let's go hunt it down."

We moved through the crowds to the tune of "Jingle Bells" being sung with a very cute interpretation. It had far more drums, and the rhythm was more alert.

"Want to dance?" he asked me. I swear, my entire body always lit up when he whispered in my ear.

I looked around and said, "Mm, too crowded."

"Then I'm going to hold that thought for later tonight."

Was this man planning sexy shenanigans *and* carols? Because I was totally up for it.

I had to ask him because it was niggling in my mind. "Xander?"

"Yeah, babe?"

"Did you pay that girl's bill at the children's hospital?" I mean, it was really his business, but I had to know. The hospital mentioned something when I last spoke to them, but they were vague. It was confidential information, of course, but I had my ways of finding out.

"Maybe."

"Xander!"

"Okay, yes. And a few more on that floor. After speaking with the nurses, I realized how a few of the families were in need, and I wanted to help them out."

I melted on the spot. To think this man, this thoughtful, caring man, did something like that made my heart soar.

We found the vendor selling sweetcorn quickly enough.

"Two pieces, please," Xander said.

"This is so cool. I've never seen it here before," I told the vendor.

He grinned. "It's my first year. I can't believe I nabbed a spot. Everyone told me that no one wants corn on Christmas, but my nan always cooked it when I was a kid. Figured there might be other people who'd enjoy it. I think I'll run out before the evening's over."

"Good for you. Merry Christmas," I said as he handed us each a piece of corn. After Xander paid him, we put salt on it and then quickly moved on.

"Mm, sweetcorn for me always tastes like summer," I exclaimed as we ate quickly. The band had changed tunes, now singing "Rudolph the Red-Nosed Reindeer." I truly liked their spin on it.

It wasn't even sinking in yet that the confectionery would still go on. I couldn't wait for Xander to tell me the changes he had in mind, but not tonight. It was Christmas Eve, and I wanted to enjoy the festivities.

When I looked up, I realized he was watching me with a grin. "When did you finish yours?"

"A few minutes ago, but you were so focused that you didn't even notice."

"I wanted to be thorough. Something you appreciate, right?" I teased.

"Very, very much." He wiggled his eyebrows.

He put his hand on my face, cupping my cheek. "Fucking hell, woman. You don't know how afraid I've been today of losing you." His raw honesty caught me by complete surprise. "Ron called me after he left the confectionery, and when I realized what was going on, I went insane from fear, and I don't say that lightly. I've never been afraid of anything in my life. I'm usually able to think through logically, lay out options, and not panic. But in that moment, all I could think was 'I can't lose this woman. I love her. I want to spend the rest of my life with her.'"

I smiled from ear to ear, then tossed the corn cob in the trash can and walked right into his arms, wrapping mine around his torso. "I love everything you're saying. And I can't believe I'm getting this super heartfelt confession on Christmas Eve here at the bonfire, of all places."

He put one palm on my lower back and the other one on my nape. "I want to be open with you, Bailey, always. There's another thing you taught me: how to wear your heart on your sleeve."

I straightened up, looking at him. "You know, I'm so proud of that."

Xander drew his head back, laughing. The sound reverberated all around me. It felt like a physical hug. "Woman, you're something else, and I'm so damn proud to be your man."

"Music to my ears." Grinning, I looked down at the half-empty basket I was carrying.

"I'll just drop these off by the small gift station they've set up so they can distribute everything to kids in need."

"Sure, let's go."

Chapter Twenty-Eight
Xander

The gift station was a small wooden cabin far away from the main square. It had no windows.

"Why is it empty?" I inquired.

"Most vendors drop off whatever is left after the celebration is over. No one usually leaves this early."

After Bailey put the basket on a table, I turned her around, kissing her deeply.

"Xander," she murmured. "I just ate corn. Let me pop a praline."

"You're delicious no matter what, Bailey."

I unbuttoned her coat, putting my hands on her waist. She instantly softened against me. Kissing her again, I walked her backward until we rested against a wall, then deepened the kiss until she rewarded me with a moan.

"I need you, Bailey. Right now."

She gasped but didn't protest. Instead, she tipped her head back, humming. I kissed down the front of her neck, pushing her jacket out of the way.

"Xander...," she half whispered, half moaned. "What if someone comes in?"

"Then we'll stop. But I'm too hungry for you."

I moved one hand under her dress. She was wearing tights. I yanked them down past her ass and then fondled her cheeks.

"Where do you need me to touch you?"

"Everywhere," she whispered. "I love it." Her voice was hoarse.

I lowered myself to my haunches, turning her around. While I traced her ass with my mouth, I brought one hand around her thigh to her pussy. *Fuuuck!* She was already touching herself. She'd slipped her hand into her panties and was applying gentle pressure. It was so damn sexy.

Pushing the fabric between her thighs to one side, I rubbed two fingers up and down her entrance, checking how wet she was. *Soaked already.* She coated my fingers instantly, so I slid one inside slowly. She shifted her weight from one leg to the other, gasping. When I slid in a second one, I could tell by the way her body was tensing up that she needed it.

I would never tire of giving pleasure to this woman, of reading her body, taking in all the cues only to give her exactly what she needed. No more, no less.

"Xander!" Her voice shook.

I was so turned on that I could barely think straight. Every time I moved my mouth from her ass up to her lower back, my cock pressed against the side of her ankle. Even though it was warm in the cabin, her skin still turned to goose bumps. I increased the rhythm of my hand, pushing my fingers in and out of her faster and faster. Gasping, she arched her back, and both her hands fell to her sides.

"Xander. Oh God, I can't..." She didn't finish the sentence, but she didn't need to. I knew what she meant. She couldn't continue like this. She needed my cock too much, and I wasn't going to withhold it from her.

I took my fingers out slowly and then rose to my feet. Bringing my hand back to her pussy, I strummed my fingers over her clit, the way she'd done before. She leaned back, dropping her head onto my shoulder. With my free hand, I quickly undid my buckle, taking the belt out as much as was necessary so I could lower my pants and boxers. I gave my cock a good squeeze, nudging her entrance, then slid in. She tightened more and more around me as I pushed in.

Fucking hell! This was too intense already. She was even closer to climaxing than I thought.

"Fuck, Bailey." I could barely breathe. The shock of the sensations coursing through me was simply too much. I forced myself to breathe in and focused on my rib cage expanding, all the while feeling her pussy clamp around my cock. I wanted to drive this woman crazy, but every time we were together, all I managed was to fall for her even more.

"I like being connected to you like this!" I wanted to stay like this for all time. I pulled back and then slammed into her again.

"I'm going to be rough, Bailey. I need it, and you're ready."

"I need it too," she said between whimpers. "I need it so bad. Please. Please."

Her words were everything I needed. I slammed into her again and again. Her body thrust forward every time, and she reached back, digging her nails into my thighs, spurring me on. She needed this even more. Then I realized she'd love another angle more.

I pushed her slightly forward. "Put your hands on the wall."

She did it instantly, and I thrust forward to the hilt.

"Xander!" Her cry was fucking delicious. I knew she was feeling me even deeper right now. I could reach her G-spot too. I moved out of her and then pushed in at a different angle.

"Touch your clit. Touch it the way you'd want me to do it." My voice was already hoarse, but I didn't care. I wasn't holding back with Bailey. I wanted her to know exactly what she did to me. To be an open book with her, to lay bare every side of me.

"Fuck," I growled as I buried myself deep inside her, the tips of her finger grazing my balls on every thrust. It only urged me on more. I thrust blindly, closing my eyes and listening to her pants and moans.

I climaxed brutally. My eyes were completely blurry, but I was hyper-aware of Bailey's cries and the way she pushed herself back into me, making the contact impact even harder. She was taking exactly what she needed, and I'd be damned if I wasn't going to give her every last bit of pleasure.

When her moans turned into a shattering, guttural groan and her pussy became even snugger around me, I stopped moving and just let her enjoy being full of my cock.

She shuddered, her body completely taut. Then she pushed herself off the wall, holding only one palm on it and resting her head on my shoulder just like before.

"I will never tire of making you come like this. You're so damn beautiful." She looked so raw and vulnerable in this moment, and it was all for me to watch and soak it all up.

"You'd better not," she murmured, "because the more I get, the more I want. Then she gasped. "Oh my God, Xander. I just realized... the ferry!"

"Shhh, I have everything under control. Let's just stay like this for a few more minutes."

Bailey

We arrived at the square right on time. I smiled and turned to Xander. He was smiling too. It was impossible not to. The atmosphere was infectious. Seeing so many people gathered here in front of St. Louis, ready to sing their hearts out, was so amazing. Some held a booklet of songs, but others weren't. Plenty knew the program by heart. I was one of them.

"Avery's winking at me," I said. She'd texted me that she was in the square waiting for us. She was looking at us with a huge grin.

"You earn so many points right now," Avery told Xander. "Look at the smile on my sister's face."

I looked from her to Xander, who nodded solemnly. "I thought you just told him where I was."

"You know what? That doesn't even matter. It's Christmas Eve."

"How about we find my family and join them?" Xander suggested.

"I can't wait to see Isabeau and Celine," Avery said. "She told me that they double-checked this afternoon that everyone can sing in tune."

I looked at Xander. "Everyone except you, huh?"

He cleared his throat. "I don't sing, babe."

My jaw dropped. Even Avery gasped, but she didn't say anything. I didn't either.

"One step at a time." I had many skills, but I couldn't turn someone into a singer in the span of thirty seconds. But he had potential for next year.

I passed a few people who were wearing red Christmas hats. Damn it. In all the frenzy, I'd forgotten my own hat at the confectionery.

"Here's the gang," Xander said, pointing to a cluster of people. It was all very tight here, but the crowd made way for us as they noticed we were heading forward in a clear direction.

Isabeau saw me first. "My darling, you brought Xander too!"

Xander rolled his eyes. "*I* brought *Bailey.*"

She was just beaming at us.

Avery waved to the group. "Hi, everyone. I think I know most of you. For those I don't, I'm Bailey's sister, Avery."

Anthony, Beckett, and Zachary greeted her, then focused on Bailey and me, flashing us shit-eating grins.

"So, rumor has it that this one took the ferry over to Algiers Point," Beckett said.

"We almost thought your assistant got it wrong," Anthony joined in.

Oh my God. They weren't going to give it a rest even on Christmas Eve. Then again, if I were them, I wouldn't either.

"How the hell would you even know?" Xander asked.

"I called Lydia because we needed to sort out some last-minute details. One thing led to another, and then I thought this was too good not to share with these two," Zachary said.

Xander raised a brow. "Is there a reason why you're not playing peace-maker right now?"

"I feel like giving you a hard time. Just woke up this morning and thought, 'How can I possibly tease our big brother?'"

"Hey, everyone," Bella cut in. "We're supposed to start soon. We should pay attention."

"See, even our niece is taking this seriously," Zachary said, the corners of his mouth twitching.

"Oh, Zachary," Adele replied. She and Remy were both dressed to the nines, just like Isabeau, David, Celine, and Felix. But the younger generation was all casual, so I didn't feel out of place.

"Avery, Bailey, let's move away from these poseurs. We can go over next to Celine and Felix," Xander said.

"You're afraid of your own brothers tonight?" I teased him.

"He always is. He just doesn't want to admit it," Zachary said.

Celine and Felix chuckled. "Your brothers are on a roll tonight. In their defense, we all had a great laugh about it as we were rehearsing," Felix said.

"Good to know."

Celine handed him a music sheet. "I brought an extra for you." She glanced at me. "You don't need one, right?"

I shook my head vehemently. "I'm up-to-date with everything."

She grinned. "Fantastic."

I took my place in line, standing as close as possible to Xander. Not only because the place was crowded, but because I genuinely craved the warmth of his body. I loved that we were sharing this together.

"You're my favorite part of this whole evening," he whispered, as though he'd read my thoughts.

"You Grinch," I murmured back, then fell completely silent because the crowd started singing. I could hear the LeBlancs clearly. They were very good. I almost felt bad for not really rehearsing.

To my astonishment, I realized Xander was singing along, too, following his sheet carefully. He winked at me but didn't stop singing.

I spotted Celine and Isabeau looking at him with wide eyes. Bella was bent at the waist, grinning. Then she glanced at me and gave me a thumbs-up.

I smiled even wider when I felt Xander's arm around my waist, pressing me against him. Even the Grinch had joined us in caroling. This was truly a Christmas miracle.

EPILOGUE
BAILEY

"Oh, yeah. Let's turn the volume up just a bit," I said to myself.

I shuffled through my playlist until it hit a song that reflected my mood. Then I indeed turned up the volume and began dancing through the confectionery's kitchen.

Could life get any better?

The summer was in full swing. I had all the windows open because it was cooking inside even though the ovens were off and the last tray of pralines had cooled long ago. I was the last person here again, but only because Xander was picking me up. We were going out for another dinner at a secret restaurant. It had become a hobby of ours. Xander kept finding out about these spots, and it was always an adventure. Granted, not all of them were as good as D's place, but we liked going nonetheless.

As I finished the very last box of pralines, I checked my messages. Zachary, Anthony, and Beckett were also stopping by.

Zachary had texted me today to ask if he could come and grab a special batch of pralines. He wouldn't say what he needed them for, but he had *very* special instructions about the filling. I made them especially for him.

As we chatted, I told him that we'd gotten some shelves for the new warehouse and that Xander was also going to stop by later. Before I knew it, he, Anthony, and Beckett had offered to come set up the shelves. I wasn't going to say no to that even though we now had a larger team. The confectionery had grown a bit over the past few months.

Xander had made deals for the pralines to be sold in several shops across the city, which meant we needed to make many more. We'd hired two kitchen helpers, and when Christmas came around, we'd have to see how we managed the charity season.

But I wasn't worried about a thing. One way or another, it would work out. I liked that growing our production, so to speak, hadn't taken the soul out of the pralines. The two women we hired were just as excited about pralines and everything we did as Avery and I were.

Since we were busier than ever with the confectionery, we didn't have as much time for our online business, but we still kept it going. It was as much a source of income as a passion project, so why shut it down?

I smiled from ear to ear as the front gate opened. I knew it was Xander before he even said, "I'm a bit early."

"That's good," I called back just as he entered the kitchen. It was so hot outside that he wasn't wearing his suit jacket, only his shirt. He'd rolled the sleeves up to his elbows.

"That is my favorite look of yours," I informed him with a grin.

He flashed a half smile. "Mine is you naked."

"Wow, that escalated quickly." I felt myself blush, although that might be from the heat. The New Orleans humidity was no joke.

There was something different about him today. He looked like he was *preparing* for something, though I couldn't explain how I knew it.

"Excited about today?" I asked as he walked toward me.

He grinned. "Yeah, I really am."

I put my hands on his chest and then moved them slowly up to his shoulders. "I never would've thought that this secret restaurant discovery was going to become one of our favorite activities."

"Honestly, I just like spending time with you. It doesn't matter what we do. We could even be wrapping pralines."

I barely bit back a laugh. "Hmm, that wouldn't be my first choice."

He smirked. "Are you insinuating that I wasn't good at it?"

"Oh, you did try your very best," I assured him. "And in a pinch, your skills will do."

"In a pinch?" he asked, stunned. "Right."

"Sorry. Did that hurt your ego?"

"Maybe. Actually, no, because it's true."

He kissed the side of my temple. The feeling that something was off intensified.

"Xander, is everything okay?"

He pulled back a bit, looking down at me. He placed his fingers on my cheek, moving in a soothing rhythm. "Yes. Why?"

"You seem a bit on edge."

"You know me well."

My stomach somersaulted. "So something *did* happen."

"You'll find out later tonight."

I looked him straight in the eye. "You're joking. You really think I'm going to be able to wait?"

"You don't have any other choice."

Ha. Well, he had another think coming. I could totally seduce him into telling me. Oh no, I couldn't because his brothers were coming.

Hmm, how best to lure the information out of him?

Oh, I knew how. I could tickle him.

I didn't give him any warning. He wasn't particularly ticklish, but I'd learned his weak spots. I went straight for his underarms, of course.

"Bailey!" He doubled over with guffaws. I first attacked his left armpit, then the right one. He attempted to take a step sideways, but I moved with him.

I was laughing, too, even though I wasn't the one being tickled. Hearing this pure joy somehow filled me with happiness, and it was contagious. My grumpy man rarely laughed out loud. He smiled, he grinned, and yes, occasionally he did laugh, but not like this. This was—

Thump, thump, thump. Something fell to the floor. I immediately stopped, glancing down.

Xander groaned. "Ah."

I didn't realize what was happening at first. Then I saw him bend down and pick up a velvet box that was open and empty. A foot away, he picked up a ring.

"Well, now the cat's out of the bag, literally," he said as he held it up between his fingers.

Instead of standing up, he simply moved onto one knee, holding up the ring.

"Xander!" I put a hand on my chest. "Oh my goodness. I'm so sorry, I didn't... Oh, you were going to propose tonight. That's why you were on edge."

He flashed me a wholehearted smile.

"I'm so sorry!"

"Babe, stop apologizing. If I can make you my fiancée a few hours earlier, that's a win for me."

I narrowed my eyes, deciding to tease him. "Make me, huh? Not ask me to be?" My heartbeat was erratic.

"You know what? This is even better. I wanted to do this properly tonight. I was actually taking you to D's. I asked them to reserve the whole restaurant for us."

I gasped. "And he agreed?"

"He likes us. But this is even better. This is the place where we first met, where I felt this unexplainable pull to you that wouldn't let go. This is where our story began."

I just nodded, my throat filling up with emotion. It was true. It all started with his visit to the confectionery.

"Since I met you, my life has become a million times better."

I laughed nervously. "That can't possibly be true."

"It is. You've filled it with so much joy and made it fuller in every possible way. And I know that life with you will be a continuous adventure, no matter if we explore new things or if we just do mundane things like wrapping pralines. I look forward to every minute of this life with you. I simply want to enjoy you everywhere there is."

He cleared his throat. It sounded as if he'd thought long and hard about this but was still coming up with things on the spot. "Before you, I never truly considered the future, but now I do. I can see us being happy for the rest of our lives, surrounded by kids."

"Yes," I said vehemently. "I can't wait to teach them how to bake too."

He chuckled. "I like how that's the first thing that came to your mind. You'll be a great mom."

I teared up a bit. "And make them fans of Christmas carols."

"Do you want to be my wife?" he asked abruptly, as if he'd suddenly just remembered that he hadn't actually asked the question.

I smiled brightly. "I will only say yes to that if you agree that I can teach our kids to properly enjoy Christmas from the get-go."

He grinned. "Babe, you've got me wrapped around your finger. Look how happy that thought makes you. Of course it's a yes."

"Then I'd love to be your wife."

He put the ring on my finger the very next second. It was gorgeous and unusual in an old-fashioned Victorian setting that I quite loved. It seemed vaguely familiar.

Xander cleared his throat. "I asked Isabeau for her ring."

I gasped. "Xander!"

"She loves you. She more than agreed to it. I knew you would be much happier with it than something I bought from the store."

I nodded and immediately bent down. I wanted to hug him, the need to be closer to him overwhelming me. But he stood up at the same time and raised me in his arms, lifting me off the floor.

I gave him a loud smooch. "I love it. I love you. I'm sorry this caught me so off guard. I want to tell you so many things, but the words won't come."

"That's okay. If you look at me like this for the rest of our lives, that's more than fine by me. You know me. I don't need words."

"I love you. I love you. I love you," I whispered between kisses. My goodness, I wanted this moment to last forever.

"Oh shit, we're cockblocking," Zachary exclaimed.

Xander immediately put me down. Zachary, Anthony, and Beckett were crowded in the doorway, grinning like crazy.

Xander frowned. "What are you three doing here?"

"I spoke to Zachary. He wanted some pralines," I told him.

"And I offered to come build the shelves for the new warehouse," Zachary explained.

"Dude, we're interrupting a moment," Anthony pointed out.

"Oh please, these two are old news," Beckett replied.

"No, there's something different," Zachary said.

I couldn't bring myself to say a word, so I just held out my hand, wiggling my fingers.

"Holy shit. Congrats!" Zachary beamed at us.

"That's Isabeau's ring." Beckett sounded stunned.

Anthony whistled. "If that's not a stamp of approval from the family, I don't know what is."

Zachary grinned from ear to ear. "All right, damn, this is bad timing. Really, brother. You proposed here?"

"I had a whole plan," Xander said, sounding mildly annoyed.

"But you decided to be spontaneous," Zachary said, then turned to me. "Just so you know, Bailey, you did do a miracle with this one. We weren't expecting it—ever."

"My God. No good deed goes unpunished in this family, does it?" Xander asked.

Anthony and Beckett laughed.

"No, dude, but that's what we had going for us," Anthony said. "You were the exacting, detail-obsessed one, and we were the ones who went with the flow."

"Hey, we still are," Zachary countered.

"Sorry to spoil this for you, brother," Beckett added, "but you are more like Xander than Anthony or I."

Zachary cocked a brow.

"Before I forget, I have your very special order of pralines." I said, holding up the box.

He smiled, taking it from me. "Thank you."

Anthony and Beckett stared at him. "Who do you need a custom order for?" Beckett asked.

"None of your business."

Just like that, I realized Zachary was hiding something. I'd thought so on the phone earlier but wasn't sure. Maybe I shouldn't have announced it in front of the others. But he did deserve some payback for teasing my man.

"I'm worrying," Anthony said. "Did Isabeau and Celine slip someone lilac perfume, and now you're going the same way as the others?"

Zachary snorted. "Nothing like that. I'm interested in investing in a... side project. A farm by the bayou. They use horses for therapy purposes. The owners are an elderly couple. Both insisted they love the LeBlanc & Broussard pralines."

"Okay, that's boring," Anthony replied.

Beckett narrowed his eyes. "Wait... you're trying to win them over? Why? Should be a slam dunk."

Zachary shook his head. "I've got competition. Someone else is interested in it. Grace Deveraux."

Xander narrowed his eyes at his brother. "Kyle and Beau Deveraux's sister? Is she trouble? I know for sure that she wasn't involved in their scheme, but nothing else."

"I don't think she's trouble like her brothers. But from what I've heard, she's every bit as arrogant and dismissive as they are."

"She's hot. I saw her recently at an event. The host went out of their way to point out that she's recently divorced and available," Beckett said, rolling his eyes.

"Doesn't matter to me," Zachary said. "Haven't even met her yet, but I'm sure I can convince her to step aside."

I cocked a brow as Xander, Anthony, and Beckett all started to give him advice at once. Oh, this was going to be a bloodbath. Orrr... sparks could fly. You just never knew when it came to the LeBlanc brothers.

Maybe I should wrap a package of pralines for Grace too. And ask Isabeau and Celine if there's any way to include lilac in sweets.

Printed in Great Britain
by Amazon